ALSO BY JOAN BRADY

GOD ON A HARLEY

HEAVEN IN HIGH GEAR

I DON'T NEED A BABY TO BE WHO I AM

To learn more about Joan Brady and her books please
go to www.JoanBradyBooks.com.

JOYRIDE

JOYRIDE

Joan Brady

Credits:
Author Photograph: Teresa Allen
Book Cover Design: Teresa Allen

To order additional copies of this book, contact:
Xlibris Corporation
1-888-795-4274
www.Xlibris.com
Orders@Xlibris.com
19512

To Teresa Allen - my friend, my colleague, my anchor

ACKNOWLEDGMENTS

Grateful acknowledgment is expressed to *God on a Harley* fans everywhere who never forgot Christine ...and who asked for more.

To learn more about Joan Brady and her books please go to www.JoanBradyBooks.com.

ONE

At four-thirty in the morning, I slipped out of bed and dressed hurriedly in the dark. Well, if you could call it that. Actually I reached for a bra, fastened it around my waist, then pulled it up and slipped my arms through the straps—all without ever removing the oversized, turquoise T-shirt I'd slept in. Next, I pulled on a pair of spandex jogging shorts while simultaneously slipping my feet into an antediluvian pair of sandals with a comfortably molded groove for my bunions.

I stole a quick glance at the dozing mass of jumbled limbs and tousled hair that was my husband—not that I should talk. To the untrained eye it appeared that he was in a near vegetative state, but I knew from years of experience that even the slightest peep out of either of the kids would send him vaulting from the bed. He's good like that.

I quietly brushed my teeth in the dim light of the streetlamp that filtered in through the bathroom window, then fumbled with a bottle of moisturizer and dabbed a thin layer of it across my face. Cupping my keys firmly in the palm of my hand so as not to jangle them, I tiptoed toward the front door, stepped over the still-sleeping dog, and let myself out into the muggy, steamy, New Jersey morning.

I crept past Jim's van of early eighties vintage and observed that it was parked at an irregular angle in the driveway. Peering through its rear window, I noticed that he had not unloaded any of the musical instruments from his gig at *Harold's Pub* last night. That could only mean one of two things; either he'd come home much later than usual and had been too tired to unpack the equipment, or he'd had a few drinks with the boys after closing.

Probably both.

As usual, I had parked my Toyota at the curb last night, as far away from our little matchbox of a house as possible. I always get up early to do the food shopping at the all-night-supermarket and I don't want the sound of my straining, rumbling engine to wake the kids. Joey is nine and Gracie, seven and, for such young children, they are both surprisingly light sleepers.

I turned the key in the ignition and automatically punched the button that turned off the radio. I knew this was probably the only time during the next twenty-four hours that I would be guaranteed absolute solitude and I intended to appreciate every second of it. I never thought I'd see the day I'd actually enjoy getting my groceries in the middle of the night like this, but this odd routine has evolved over the years into a sacred ritual for me, a sort of rendezvous with myself.

I tied my hair back with a covered elastic band, then pulled out onto the still dark and deserted streets. At the top of the hill I turned right by a sign that said 'Hurry Back to Neptune City' which always amuses me since only a few blocks away is another one that reads, 'Welcome to Neptune City'. Like most of the tiny coastal towns that punctuate the Jersey shore, if you sneeze more than a few times while driving, you could literally pass through whole communities without ever knowing it.

The miniscule towns that line the coast are like so many pieces of a complicated jigsaw puzzle. The Jersey shore often gets overlooked in the gigantic and somewhat oppressive shadow of the three major cities surrounding it: Philadelphia to the west, New York City to the

north, and Atlantic City to the south, not to
mention our nation's capitol a little further to
the south. Personally, I have always believed that
it takes a certain level of sophistication to truly
appreciate the nuances offered by this quaint
and lovely area. For instance, it is mostly the
elderly who populate the nearby municipality
of Ocean Grove; hence the nickname 'Ocean
Grave' has emerged. So, even if there are some
quirky names for these towns, there is nothing
unrefined about the way the sun lifts its
smoldering head above the horizon in Avon-by-
the-Sea, or the way the moon casts a platinum
path across the water toward the boardwalk in
Bradley Beach, or the way the stars decorate the
clear and un-polluted skies above Neptune City.

These are the thoughts I entertained as I
drove unhurriedly toward the bright lights of
our newly opened, world-class supermarket
called 'Shop-Well'. In spite of the chronic and
severe state of sleep deprivation in which I live,
this time of morning seems to awaken a shy and
reserved piece of my soul. It feels like I have the
whole world to myself, along with a little
uninterrupted time to think. The day is still a
newborn at this hour, full of peace, promise,
and potential—all of which I remember feeling
a million years ago when I was young and single.

I was thirty-eight years old when I got
married, hardly a child bride, so I know I had a

life other than the tightly scheduled and sometimes frantic one I now share with Jim and the kids. I just can't seem to remember very much of it. Marriage and motherhood have somehow drastically sped up the pace of my days to the point where life has just become one big blur of activity.

Believe me when I tell you that a lot of interesting things happened during those first thirty-eight years of my existence; things I've never really told anyone about. What little I still remember seems almost surreal now, like a vaguely familiar dream. I sometimes wonder if any of it ever really happened.

I'd gone through a lengthy and painful period of dating all kinds of men back then—mostly the wrong kind—before finally stumbling upon Jim MaGuire, a promising musician of local fame. I'd bought the one and only CD he'd ever cut when I'd heard it playing in a music store down by the beach one night. I had been moved and deeply touched by the sheer beauty of it. Though I'd never even heard of Jim MaGuire up until then, I'd felt instinctually drawn to him through his music, like a homing pigeon that suddenly found itself within landing distance of its final destination.

At the time, I worked the three-to-eleven shift at Valley Community Hospital and lived in a rented and romantic cottage on the beach. I subscribed to the 'less is more' philosophy back then and didn't own much of anything. The way I saw it, anything that didn't fit into the back seat of my car, pretty much owned me. Amazingly, I didn't even have an alarm clock in those days. I figured if I couldn't get up in time to work the three to eleven shift, I had far bigger problems than a minimalist lifestyle. The word 'responsibility' only had meaning during the thirty-two-hour, part-time workweek I'd chosen for myself. I'd been completely oblivious then to the concepts of mortgages, braces, and college funds—things that would eventually come to consume me.

I used to show up around midnight at a popular little joint called *The Cave* where Jim and his saxophone were frequently the featured entertainment. I fell in love with Jim's music long before I ever actually met him, which at the time, I considered to be a very good sign. I mean, music comes from a place in the soul, so in a way I figured I'd heard Jim's soul calling to mine through his music and it all just seemed so right. Not to sound corny or anything, but when the priest pronounced us man and wife, chills actually ran up my spine because I had the most incredible feeling that God, Himself, had sanctioned this marriage.

After officially becoming Mrs. James MaGuire, I had thought the hardest part was over. It's embarrassing to admit, but I guess I just presumed everything would be fine once I had married the man I loved. I was convinced that finally finding my soul mate was the key to a successful marriage. Once I had cleared that hurdle, I naively believed that all the other components of our relationship—things like job, money, and family—would simply fall into place and fit together into one big, happy collage called 'Our Marriage'. I didn't understand then that finding the right partner is only a very small part of what makes a relationship work. Instead, I had believed with all my heart that romantic love was the answer to absolutely everything, and that being married meant I would never be lonely again.

How wrong I was.

Jim's career never took off quite the way the music pundits around the shore had predicted it would. Like a fickle lover, audiences gradually turned their attentions to the younger, more robust rockers who had sprouted up in Jim's gentle shadow. Though he claimed he'd never shared everyone's lofty expectations of fame and fortune in the first place, I couldn't help but notice a subtle, yet significant, shift in my husband's demeanor. I watched a dimmer switch take hold in his eyes the day he joined a local band and began playing gigs wherever he could get them.

By the end of our first year of marriage, I
became increasingly aware of a swift current
of disillusionment that tugged on the edges of
Jim's confidence and threatened to drown his
artistic genius. I heard his disappointment lying
heavy on the notes he blew through his
saxophone, felt it on his fingertips when he
touched me in ways which once had left me
weak, and tasted it on the room-temperature
kisses that had long since become as mediocre
as his music now.

Jim once told me that I keep a thin film
between us—a veil that a man, not even a
husband, can penetrate. At first I disagreed;
wanted to convince myself it wasn't true. But
now I guess I have to admit that I do withhold a
small piece of myself. Like my own heartbeat, it
is something that belongs exclusively to me and
I fear that if I expose it to the whims of another
human being, I might actually die. Perhaps that
was part of the problem too.

Looking back over the years, I'd have to say
that language was at the very root of our
problems. Jim speaks the vernacular of self-
expression, musical instruments, and artistic
freedom, while I understand only the parlance
of responsibility, productivity, and consequences.
Inevitably, I suppose, we became like two
foreigners in this territory called 'us', each
speaking a different dialect and neither achieving

any kind of meaningful communication with the other.

Eventually, and without saying very much about it, Jim began supplementing our income by giving music lessons in our home to some of the kids from the wealthy, neighboring town of Spring Lake. I gave birth to Joey right around that time, but even the arrival of our healthy, hearty son did little to lift the flagging spirits of this familiar stranger to whom I was married.

I suppose the real hard evidence that our relationship was in demise came about two years later in the bleak, dog-tired weeks after Gracie was born. It became apparent then that, though we had agreed that I would be a stay-at-home-Mom, something had to be done about our seriously ailing finances. That 'something' turned out to be a full-time nursing position for me back at Valley Community Hospital. I was a mere six weeks post-partum when I hauled myself back to work, still swollen, sore, and lactating.

I took a position on the day shift on the Orthopedic unit, commonly known as the 'Elephant's Graveyard' and I have been working there ever since. There are always openings on this floor because it encompasses one of the least appealing types of nursing care there is; the backbreaking work of turning and lifting elderly patients with broken hips. This is the place where nurses earn their bunions and bad backs and I had attained both long ago. At forty-one, I'd felt I was far too old for this type of work, but I also knew I had no choice.

I suppose I became a nurse the same way I'd become a mother: it just seemed like the natural thing to do. I'd felt it was expected of me and so, never questioned it, at least, not until I realized I was going to have to do both simultaneously. In all honesty, I think that is when the first tiny seeds of resentment began to stir in some dark and moldy crevice in the general vicinity of my stomach.

I walked the floors during the late night hours with a colicky, screeching infant daughter, while Jim played in his band in the name of making a living. His idea of work meant playing the music that he loved and charming the crowd of young and starry-eyed females who fantasized about bagging a 'rock star'.

Like I used to do.

I watched the clock continuously during those days, counting the minutes till he'd get home. The second he walked through the door, I'd hand the baby over to him so I could collapse onto the bed for a few hours of exhausted and much needed sleep before getting up at four-thirty and doing it all over again.

Grace always settled down quickly in her father's arms and for some reason I found that particularly annoying. Within only minutes, I would feel the bed sloping down on Jim's side as he crawled in beside me, immediately falling into a seemingly peaceful and untroubled sleep while I lay awake, uneasy and disturbed. I think that's when I realized that the passion had evaporated from our marriage and that I wasn't at all sure where it had gone. All I knew was that I felt sad and tired and left out. The fire had gone out in our relationship and I found myself wondering whether or not I had the energy or the will to rebuild it.

It has been that way for seven years now. We don't fight. Well, not really. We just seem to have worked out a system that the biology books would probably refer to as 'symbiotic'. Somehow, we survive financially and the kids seem to be unaware that each of their parents is walking around with a great big, sucking chest wound where a heart used to beat.

So, here I was again, preparing to cruise the aisles of the all-night supermarket like a mother lion hunting for breakfast for her young. There is something instinctual, almost primitive, which kicks in the moment I pull into the Shop-Well parking lot and go through a mental list of the supplies Jim and my little cubs will need for the morning.

Like mates and mothers of most species, I am quick to put my own needs at the tail end of the list so that I can provide for my family first.

If anything is overlooked, or if I am just too
damn tired to finish shopping, at least I can rest
assured that I will not be the one to throw a
temper tantrum or shed a tear of disappointment
over a missing pair of panty hose or a forgotten
box of tampons. For some reason, that knowledge
gives me great comfort.

I turned left into the driveway and drove
slowly past the handicapped spaces and the
motorcycles that were parked by the front
entrance of the store. A wave of nostalgia took
me by surprise, hitting me hard. Jim used to
have a motorcycle, a Harley-Davidson in fact.
As if on cue, I noticed a longhaired man stuffing
a single bag of groceries into the leather pouch
on the backside of his bike. Satisfied that his
purchases were secure, he donned a helmet and
ignited the powerful engine of that beautiful
machine. His girlfriend climbed on behind him
and slipped her young, health-club-toned arms
around the man's hard, muscular waist. He revved
the engine and she hung on tight as they sprang
away from the curb like a crouching, wild animal
on the attack. A thrill ran through me. That
used to be me, I thought wistfully. A million
years and twenty pounds ago maybe, but that
used to be Jim and me.

A strong memory wafted past me then like
an alluring perfume that made me perk up and
take notice, then dissolved into the muggy, still

air. For one lovely and ephemeral moment, I remembered what it was like to be fit, trim, well rested, and excited about life. How had I lost that feeling and where was it hiding? Furthermore, since I'd probably never be able to afford the time or the money to join a health club ever again, was it even possible to recapture that optimism and sense of well being? I supposed, like so many other changes in my life, I should just try to accept my aging body with a little dignity.

I sighed heavily and parked my tired, old Toyota in a spot that was well within screaming distance of the scrawny security guard who was stationed at the front entrance of the store. For some reason, parking this close to the lighted doorway always gives me a sense of safety, though more than likely, a false one. Realistically, if someone actually attacked me, I would not expect the post-pubescent teenager (who was being paid minimum wage to wear a weaponless, blue uniform) to throw himself into the path of danger for me. In fact, my guess is that my nurturing and maternal instincts would suddenly kick in and *I* would end up defending *him*.

I clambered out of the car, locked it, and headed toward the store. I've just been a nurse and a mother too long, I decided.

I passed another couple emerging from the

store, jointly pushing a shopping cart toward their car. Their conversation was animated and punctuated with laughter, and I wondered what could possibly be so amusing at this ungodly hour. The man opened the trunk, tossed a few bags inside, then walked around to the passenger side and opened the door for the woman.

I remembered when men used to do that for me.

I continued on toward the automatic doors that obediently slid open upon my approach. That is when it occurred to me that these were the only kind of doors that ever got held for me any more.

While the electronic eye politely waited for me to pass through, I caught a glimpse of the reflection of a dowdy, slightly overweight, middle-age woman walking through the entryway and, to my horror, realized that it was me.

Numbly, I wrestled a cart from the row stacked just outside of the doors and shoved it inside. Surely that reflection had just been a distortion. There probably was a defect in the cheap glass they use, I told myself.

I aimed the cart toward the packaged carrots and salads that lined the shelves of the produce aisle. I moved a few of them aside and tentatively glanced into the smudged and frosted mirror behind them. My heart sank. It was true. The same frumpy, fatigued woman from the glass doors out front stared back at me.

Inexplicably, I found myself sobbing uncontrollably in the middle of the produce aisle . . . in the middle of the night . . . in the middle of my life.

TWO

I pulled myself together just in time to feign a cold as a teenaged stock boy turned the corner and sauntered toward me, pushing a wet mop. As if to prove my innocence, I practiced a skill known only to mothers and produced a tissue seemingly out of nowhere. With exaggerated emphasis, I blew my nose as though I were apparently suffering from some odd strain of summer flu.

The stock boy smiled sympathetically. "Tylenol and Nyquil are in aisle sixteen," he offered.

I nodded. "Thanks. That's just where I was heading," I lied.

Obliged to live up to the lie now, I turned my cart in the direction of the 'cold and flu' aisle, grateful that my act had apparently been convincing enough to dupe a sixteen-year-old. But what if I hadn't been able to get a grip fast enough, I wondered. What if I'd just stood there blubbering like the exhausted, defeated, middle-aged-woman-having-a-meltdown that I was? What then? Would the stock boy's job have required him to call 911? I could just hear him telling the operator that the frumpy looking woman in the produce aisle was having a nervous breakdown among the carrots, basil, and spinach.

Here I was, I thought, forty-eight years old and completely disillusioned with my job, my marriage, and, worst of all, myself. I still remember making a list one time of the three biggest problems in my life and they were: men, my weight, and my job. That was about twelve years ago and the sad thing is that the list is still pretty much the same today, except for the addition of a fourth major issue which is 'lack of time'.

Listlessly, I trudged along the brightly lit linoleum floors of the Shop-Well examining my present state of mind and trying to make some sense of it. With abject determination, I decided to sort through the list yet again, beginning with my job. The truth is that I felt I had been cornered into a career that has been drastically and catastrophically changed by the advent of managed care or, as I like to call it, 'conveyor-belt-medicine'. In my opinion, not only has the health care system taken the very heart out of the nursing profession, but the job now also requires the mental and physical stamina of a person half my age—who also does triathlons on the side. Realistically, how much longer could I expect to function in that capacity?

Then there is the added indignity of knowing that the minute I show any sign of weakness, there will be an eager young nurse from a third world country just waiting to take my place . . . for lower pay, of course. In a way, it's almost funny. The same situation that makes me feel used and exploited will eventually make some poor, immigrant nurse feel rich beyond her wildest dreams. Valley Community Hospital counts on that.

And then there is the matter of my ever-fluctuating weight. Actually, it doesn't really fluctuate any more, it just seems to steadily increase these days. I hate to use the old pregnancy excuse, but it is an indisputable fact that, after twice giving birth at a somewhat mature age, my metabolism has turned against me. Not that it was ever much of a friend in the first place, but at least it was a lot easier to shed a few pounds in the years before I became a middle-aged mother. Of course, taking the kids to

McDonald's on pit stops between activities, and then eating cafeteria food at work hasn't exactly helped matters. Sometimes food is my only comfort, especially when I'm tired, which is all the time.

I avoid looking at pictures of myself when I was fit and trim, which means that our wedding album is stashed out of sight somewhere, probably in the garage or up in the attic. I'm not sure which, and I don't really care. Not only are these extra pounds depressing, they're downright embarrassing.

I think Jim finally gets it that my weight is a forbidden topic of conversation. He is aware of how sensitive I am about the subject and wisely never mentions it. Of course, he hasn't touched me in an awfully long time either. The scary thing is that I'm kind of relieved. Somewhere along the way, Jim metamorphosed from a husband into a 'significant other', a term I've only recently come to appreciate.

So, how did this happen? How had Jim and I become so hopelessly distant from one another? In a way, I suppose it was inevitable for our marriage to be on the rocks. After all, what is the divorce rate these days? Fifty per cent, isn't it? So I guess I shouldn't have been so shocked that things weren't working out the way I had envisioned them ten years ago on my wedding day. Up until that time, I had pictured married life as an abundant stream of love, lust, and bliss. I'd had no idea that the stream would feed into an ocean of exhaustion, obesity, and resentment.

I remembered back to when I was single and how my married friends were always touting the praises of matrimony as if it were a secret club that I should want to join. Now, I wondered if it had all been a big practical joke. I didn't know of any married couples these days that I truly believed to be happy.

Shaking my head in quiet resignation, I plodded onward past the bins of melons and plums. Life is just about making ends meet, keeping the house and family in some kind of order, and getting groceries in the middle of the night, I decided. Amen. End of story.

Sniffling, I trudged past neatly stacked mountains of potatoes and bananas silently wondering what was wrong with me. Why was I walking around like a raw nerve? Years of working in hospitals had proved beyond a doubt that plenty of people suffered through far greater problems than chronic fatigue and a deteriorating marriage, yet I didn't see anyone else traipsing through the store with tears in their eyes.

Then again, maybe I just never looked hard enough.

On that note, I scanned my surroundings and had to admit that it was pretty hard to feel like a misfit in this particular environment. I noticed a morbidly obese woman swipe a king-size Hershey bar from the candy shelf and then quickly hide it among the 'healthy' items in her cart when she saw me looking—as if I had any room to talk about sugar addictions. I moved on and caught a glimpse of a tattooed and slovenly-dressed young couple at the far end of the bread aisle. Oblivious to the elderly woman who was rooting through the day-old bagels right beside them, the two were hanging all over each other and making out as if they were in a secluded, romantic park.

I decided the English muffins on my list could wait.

There's definitely something about this late night hour, I thought, that attracts an eclectic element to the supermarket. They tend to be the kind of people who dwell only on the fringes of mainstream society. Sometimes I actually make a game of diagnosing the more blatant ailments that plague the diverse lives of these late night shoppers; schizophrenia, alcohol and drug abuse, loneliness, diabetes, depression and so forth. It seems I never stop being a nurse. I wish I could quit doing this, but from force of habit, I can't seem to resist the urge to mentally evaluate and treat everyone's problems—except for my own, that is.

As if to prove the point, two girls in miniskirts

and leather boots were perusing the 'feminine products' aisle when I passed by. I could see from ten feet away that they were both high on something, but this time a surprising flash of envy washed over me. How nice it must be to just zone out and escape the realities of life, I thought. Just as quickly, however, Christine Moore MaGuire, registered nurse and mother of two, chided me from some deep and disciplined corner of my psyche, mentally slapping me back to my senses as I continued on my excursion through the aisles.

Other than the absurdity of the hour and the eccentricities of the patrons, the only real problem I find shopping at this time is the inaccessibility of certain products. The store uses this quiet lull to re-stock shelves, frequently roping off large areas in order to do so. This forces determined and sometimes desperate customers like me to squeeze past cones and crawl over various barricades to reach the items that they need.

I was relieved to see that the 'digestive aids' section was still open, though several stacks of heavy cartons were randomly piled in front of the merchandise. I turned my cart in and began rummaging around for an antacid, not for me, but for the dog. Yes, the dog. She has inflammatory bowel disease and, even though the medicine is expensive and I am the only one who remembers to give it to her, I have learned the hard way not to ever let her miss a dose.

That reminded me; I needed stain remover for the carpets.

I pulled the ever-present pen from above my ear and added *Karpet Klean* to the list. That's when a funny thing happened. I got the distinct impression that someone was standing behind me. I turned, but there was no one in sight. Shrugging, I reached for the bottle of antacid and tossed it into the cart. Again, a strange sort of presence permeated my personal space and this time, I even thought I heard footsteps, but when I turned around, the aisle was completely vacant.

That struck me as odd because Jim is always telling me that I am the least observant person he has ever known and I'd have to admit he's probably right. I'm usually so focused on whatever task I am performing at the moment, that I tend to have a sort of tunnel vision. Once, Jim came home with a black eye after being caught in the crossfire of a barroom brawl that broke out while he was playing in the band. It took me three hours the next morning to finally notice the shiner beneath his right eye.

So why was I sensing something now that clearly wasn't there? It made no sense. Then a terrible thought struck me. During a recent in-service on personal safety at the hospital, a detective from Bradley Beach had lectured us on sexual predators and how nurses are often the targets of such crimes. He'd said that our tendencies to be helpful and nurturing often made us vulnerable to such attacks. I wondered now if I was giving off some kind of 'nurse vibe' to whatever nut-case might be lurking in these deserted aisles. Either that, or I figured I must be closer to cracking than I thought.

I had no time for nervous breakdowns though, and dutifully went back to perusing the shelves. It occurred to me that the dog's left ear smelled funny again and I assumed it was another fungal infection, no doubt. Picturing yet another visit to the vet that we simply could not afford, I tried to think of a home-remedy that might be effective. On a whim, I eyed a tube of Monostat on the next shelf. Figuring that a fungus is a fungus, I was just about to drop the tube into the cart when a thundering crash at the end of the aisle made my blood run cold, momentarily paralyzing me.

By the time I could bring myself to look, an elderly man was lying on the floor near the checkout stand, his arms and legs splayed in all different directions. A small crowd of stunned spectators had already begun to gather, as the man lay motionless and unresponsive on the freshly mopped linoleum. With morbid curiosity, a small group of onlookers peered into his ashen and lifeless face as though waiting for some kind of spontaneous or miraculous recovery. Next, a frail and panic-stricken woman dropped to her knees on the floor beside the man. She clenched one of his puffy, bloated hands inside both of hers and alternated between yelling into the man's face for him to wake up and demanding that someone in the crowd help her.

"I'm a nurse," I heard myself announce as I worked my way through the group of bystanders. I knelt beside the hysterical woman who was now sprawled across the unconscious man's body. "What's his name?" I demanded, plunging my fingers into the man's neck to feel for a carotid pulse.

"Harry," the wrinkled little woman whimpered as she crawled off of him. "He's my Harry."

I grabbed old Harry by the shoulders and shook him hard. "Harry! Harry! Are you all right?" I hollered just the way the Basic Life Support books tell you to and, for the very first time, I didn't feel ridiculous saying those words. This wasn't a practice session on a plastic dummy called 'Annie': this was the real thing.

Harry didn't reply and his pulse wasn't answering either. I put my ear next to Harry's nose and mouth and watched his chest for any hint of respirations. There were none.

"Okay, somebody call 911!" I shouted at

several pairs of shoes that were in my field of vision. I knew I had to give two quick breaths of air before starting chest compressions, but when I looked at the blue and lifeless lips, saliva was bubbling from them and I hesitated.

For some crazy reason, I noticed a spotless pair of white Nike athletic shoes that stood out from all the sandals, flip-flops, and clogs surrounding me. I pointed to the white Nikes with one hand, while loosening Harry's collar with the other. "You!" I demanded without bothering to look at the face, "Go get me a gauze pad! They're right there in aisle sixteen. Hurry!"

The shoes remained stationary. "I don't think you have to be concerned about a little saliva," the owner of the Nikes said calmly, "I know this man and he doesn't have any contagious diseases."

I couldn't believe what I was hearing! I wanted to cut this guy to ribbons with some kind of condescending remark, but my main priority at the moment was to take care of old Harry. Sarcastic comments would have to take a back seat for now.

Someone in the crowd handed me a neatly folded, linen handkerchief, which I placed over Harry's lips and then began mouth-to-mouth resuscitation. The paramedics arrived within mere minutes and took over. After several harrowing moments, they had him breathing again and his color became a passable shade of pink. The crowd dispersed and Harry was carted off to the hospital, his terrified little wife still clutching his hand.

Just as quickly as it had begun, the commotion was completely over now, and all I could think about was paying for my groceries so I could get home in time to start breakfast for the kids and get myself off to work on time. Like the seasoned veteran that I am, I consciously distanced my emotions from the drama and deliberately gave no further thought to what had just happened.

I retrieved my cart from the middle of the aisle where I had left it, and calmly proceeded to the checkout stand. I tried to maintain a non-committal demeanor, as if facing death was a daily occurrence, which in my case, it is. I took my place in line behind an attractive young woman with long, silky hair and a bathing suit top that overflowed with tanned, toned breasts. Apparently she had come out this early in the morning to buy a magazine, a bouquet of fresh flowers, and a quart of ice cream; luxuries that I no longer allowed myself.

I was fascinated by the effect her presence had on the male clerk at the register and the boy who bagged the groceries. The two of them began falling all over themselves to make small talk with her as the rest of us less endowed customers stood waiting our turns. The bag-boy took painstaking care in arranging the young woman's items just so in the plastic bag, and then offered to carry her 'packages' to the car for her. Graciously, she granted him that privilege.

I moved up in line and began emptying the contents of my cart onto the counter. Not surprisingly, my purchases, though greater in bulk and in number, were added up and packed into bags with impressive efficiency. Apparently, saving someone's life doesn't warrant quite as much acclaim as being young and beautiful does. What power young girls have, I thought. Too bad so many of them don't realize it until it's too late. Suddenly, I wanted another chance at being young. I wanted to be Christine Moore again, no raving beauty perhaps, but happy and vital and alive.

I missed her.

My thoughts were interrupted by a half-hearted offer from the cashier to have my bags carried to the car. In a stand for independence and dignity I declined. The bag-boy actually looked relieved.

When the automatic doors opened this time, they revealed a sky that was a muted shade of mauve. The sun wasn't quite up as I emerged into the steamy, humid dawn, but the early morning joggers were. I spotted a few of them as they cut through the parking lot on padded, noiseless shoes, running with a grace known only to trained athletes, their heavy breathing softly punctuating the stillness of the air.

I took a moment and immersed myself in the peace and quiet of the pre-dawn loveliness. I tried to capture some of the solace surrounding me so that I could call upon it later in the day when I would have to shift gears and go at full throttle through the chaos of a hectic orthopedic unit on the day shift.

That's when that same funny feeling washed over me again.

I scanned the parking lot carefully before venturing any further, but again, I noticed nothing out of the ordinary. Disconcerted, I pushed the shopping cart toward my Toyota and rested it carefully beside the rear bumper, chastising myself for being paranoid now. I popped the trunk and, with a sense of urgency, began loading the bags inside as quickly as possible.

The last bag somehow fell out of my hands, spilling its contents onto the ground. Six plastic yogurt containers began rolling in different directions and I bent down to grab the two that were headed toward the underside of my car. My fingers scraped the asphalt as I reached for the renegade containers and suddenly, what I saw beside them stopped my heart.

Spotless, white, Nike athletic shoes were firmly planted mere inches from my rambling hands and I heard myself emit a frightened little gasp. I had no doubt the shoes were attached to the same person who had refused to get the gauze pads for me only minutes earlier.

My heart hammered in my chest while my gaze traveled upward past the jeans, the leather belt, the white T-shirt, and finally came to rest upon a pair of dark and bottomless, brown eyes that were both magnificent and familiar.

I straightened my shoulders and faced him squarely in the luminescent light of dawn. Neither of us made any attempt to move. Then, placidly, he extended his large and graceful hand toward me as he took in my startled expression. His curvy lips expanded into a gentle smile, but he said nothing.

"Joe," I whispered hoarsely, "where the heck have you been?"

THREE

Perhaps I should explain. I've never told anyone about this, but I guess maybe it's time now.

You could say that Joe is actually—well—more *evolved* than the rest of us. I met him a little over ten years ago when I discovered that my non-committal boyfriend of three years, Doctor Greg Anderson, had married someone else shortly after our break-up. I was not aware of this because I had immediately gone out to the west coast to lick my wounds and try to start over. I had made it clear to friends and family alike that I never wanted to hear Greg's name again or to know anything about him. Several years later, when I thought I was finally over him, I'd come back to New Jersey only to run into a more attractive, successful, and settled-down version of him in the hospital cafeteria. I'd made a total fool of myself that night by entertaining thoughts of a romantic reunion before I finally noticed the wedding band on his left hand. The real kick in the teeth was that his now-wife had once been a colleague of mine, one of whom I'd never been particularly fond.

The short version is that I'd gone down to the beach to have a good cry when I got off duty that night, and I ran into this gorgeous, Harley-Davidson-riding man who turned out to be Joe. Oh, and one more thing; Joe turned out to be God. I'm not kidding. I didn't believe it at first either, but it's true. He did all kinds of things to prove it to me, not the least of which was healing my broken heart, showing me how to be happy again, and finding me a husband.

Talk about performing miracles.

He'd said I could call him anything I wanted and he gave me a list of suggestions that included things like *Universal Force, God, Higher Power, Joe*, you know, that sort of thing. Since I am what can only be described as a Catholic-school-casualty, I told him that I preferred just plain old 'Joe' because it sounds so much less intimidating than the others. He graciously agreed. Joe definitely wasn't on a power trip and I liked that. In fact, I'd fallen a little bit in love with him during our time together, though it still makes me uncomfortable to admit that.

Back then, Joe had told me that he was on a sort of mission to spend a little quality time with each and every person on earth, instead of addressing the masses as had been his long and sad history. Nowadays, he went around giving each individual a customized set of guidelines that were pertinent to only that particular person. On the last night I saw him, Joe had actually had my personal guidelines etched into a little gold charm that he presented to me just before he left.

A few years later, Gracie, my daughter, pulled it out of my jewelry box one day when she was a toddler. On a whim, she flushed it down the toilet when Jim, who was supposed to be watching her, wasn't looking. I was heartbroken and Jim couldn't understand why I was so upset over a tiny, gold charm. Like I said, I've never told anyone about this until now because they'd probably think I was hallucinating and have me locked up. Jim kept asking me why I was so distraught, but I never told him. He kept offering to buy me a new charm—any kind I wanted—if I would just stop obsessing over the lost one and making him feel bad. I told him it could never be replaced and that was that. Neither of us ever mentioned it again. I didn't think I'd ever see Joe again and once I no longer had any tangible proof of his existence, I sort of let myself slip into believing that maybe I had just dreamed up the whole experience.

Joe always did have a way of keeping me on the straight and narrow though, and now, I couldn't believe that I was looking into his beautiful, serene face again, thrilled beyond belief that he was back. He was as striking as ever, tall and slim with new flecks of silver in his otherwise jet black hair that he still wore rakishly long. Just like the first night I'd met him, his large, elegant hand was outstretched, beckoning me to take it. Timidly, I placed my trembling hand inside of his and immediately, I got a feeling that can only be described as being home again. Tenderly, Joe kissed my fingers and a wave of sheer joy rippled through me.

Suddenly, I wanted Joe to embrace me in those powerful arms of his and to keep me safe from everything that was hurting me. I wanted to melt into him, to rest my head against his heart and hear the ocean waves again like I had the first night I'd met him.

But I didn't dare.

I had no idea what was appropriate and what wasn't, and so I chose to wait and watch. I stood there with my hand curled happily inside of his, searching for any sign that it was still okay to embrace him.

Then I remembered something and, of all

the pressing issues in my life, for some crazy reason the first thing I chose to say was, "Why wouldn't you get me those gauze pads I asked for?"

Joe laughed out loud at that. "Oh, Christine," he said without even a trace of annoyance, "You're still so filled with fear and distrust, aren't you?"

"Well, you would be too," I retorted, "if you saw all the contagious stuff I work with day in and day out."

Again, Joe laughed. "I know," he said reassuringly, "but you forget. I know how these things turn out long before they actually happen. I was just trying to save you some time and some worry, that's all. I knew Harry didn't have any, oh, what do you call them again?"

"Risk factors," I filled in for him.

"Right, risk factors. That's it."

"Well, how was I supposed to know you had any credibility?" I shot back. I was mildly aware of my defensive tone, but I continued anyway. "I was down there on the floor talking to a bunch of feet. Besides, I have two children now and I don't want to bring anything home to them, you know."

"Okay," Joe conceded, "you're right to be concerned. I'm glad to see the old maternal instinct I installed is working properly. By the way, nice job in there."

"Actually, I screwed up," I admitted a little sheepishly. "You're supposed to listen for breath sounds first before feeling for a pulse. I guess I was a little nervous. I would have lost points for that at work."

Joe rolled his eyes and loosened his grip on my hand, shoving both of his own hands deep into the pockets of his jeans. He hesitated for a moment and then looked directly into my eyes. "You're right," he finally said. "Just because you saved a life in there doesn't mean you should cut yourself any slack, right?"

I winced because I knew where this was going. I've never been comfortable giving myself credit for much of anything. For some reason (which I strongly suspect has something to do with my parochial school education), I have always been far more comfortable with criticism than with compliments. I had a feeling that Joe was about to point that out to me.

"Really, Christine," he said, picking up both of my hands this time, "don't you ever get tired of beating yourself up?"

I laughed. "Apparently not."

Heavy silence hung like a velvet curtain between us and, as usual, Joe waited for me to decide what more needed to be said. "Oh, Joe," I finally blurted out, shaking my head, "I guess I just feel like such a failure."

"Because you saved a man's life in there?" he asked tenderly, and there was not even the slightest hint of sarcasm in those words.

"No. Because I've let you down," I confessed. "Because I've done so much backsliding since the last time we were together. I mean, how many people actually get God, Himself, as a personal mentor? And even with that huge advantage, I've made myself miserable again anyway. I'm embarrassed, I guess. That's all."

Joe didn't agree or disagree. "I see," he said. That's all, just 'I see'.

I didn't look him in the eye, didn't want to. Instead, I focused on his hands, their warmth, their smoothness, their disproportionately large size which I supposed you would need if you were always holding peoples' troubles in your palm.

I watched a flock of sparrows come in for a landing on the asphalt right behind him, and they began unceremoniously eating the contents of a discarded bag of popcorn. Though several of the tiny birds were only inches from Joe's feet, they seemed to sense no threat from him at all and casually went about their business, confident that they could let their guard down while they were around him.

I knew the feeling.

"There's something else I need to say," I murmured softly.

Joe waited patiently for me to unload my fears and concerns on him and I didn't disappoint him. Words began spilling from my mouth so fast that I forgot to take a breath in between. This was important stuff and I had to get it out before I lost my nerve.

"I'm afraid you'll get tired of helping me," I began in a trembling voice. "I mean, I really did practice all those great principles you taught me back when I was still single, but then I married Jim and before I knew it, the kids came along and somehow, I just put all those important lessons on the back burner and forgot about them till, all of a sudden, they didn't seem real to me anymore." I drew in a deep and much needed breath at that point. "So, that's why I'm afraid maybe you'll get frustrated and impatient with me," I concluded. "Because I'm such a slow learner, I mean."

"I see."

He stayed quiet again just in case there was anything else I wanted to add to that little tirade. Satisfied that there wasn't, he went on.

"Seems to me you're the only one who gets impatient with you," he said with genuine sincerity. "Have you noticed that?"

I snorted at that. "You haven't been hanging around with my husband and kids, I see."

He didn't get it. "Christine, there's nothing wrong with your capacity for learning," he assured me, ignoring my last comment. "Spiritual enlightenment isn't a race or a contest. The fact is, it's a whole lot easier to remember how to take care of yourself and how to be happy when you're the only one you have to worry about. It gets a lot more complicated when you add the demands of a family on top of everything else. Don't you see? You did so well with those principles when you were single, that I moved you up a notch to a slightly more challenging level. You might actually think of it as a promotion of sorts."

I felt as though a hundred pounds of dead weight had just been lifted off my shoulders. I should have known there would be no chastisement or criticism from Joe. He was such a kind and loving creature, and it seemed to me that his top priority always had something to do with making me feel better. Now, do you see why I fall in love with this man every time I encounter him? Where do you find compassion and understanding and perfect love like that? How could anyone *not* love this man?

"*All* love is perfect," Joe stated matter-of-factly and I remembered that he could hear my thoughts. That used to freak me out when I'd first met him, but now it appeared I was a little more comfortable with it. That showed at least some progress on my part, I supposed.

"But I'm so afraid, Joe," I heard myself blurt out and I was surprised to hear a little sob erupt from somewhere deep inside of me. Without permission, a flood of tears began flowing down my face. "I'm so afraid sometimes that I've screwed everything up," I cried. "You're right, of course. I am the one who gets impatient and frustrated, and not just with myself. I get grumpy and annoyed with the kids sometimes and I feel so guilty about that." I gulped past the lump of yet-to-be-shed tears in my throat. "I mean, I love Joey and Gracie so much, but I'm afraid maybe they don't know it because I'm always so uptight and tired and busy."

Joe smiled sympathetically. "Everything's going to be all right, Christine," he said with great confidence. Then he surprised me by pulling me close to him. I reveled in the moment and breathed in the familiar scent of him as though I'd been starving for it and, in a way, I was. Like the little sparrows at his feet, I allowed myself to relax completely in Joe's reassuring presence. "Trust me, okay?" I heard him murmur into my hair.

That's when I felt something stir in the pit of my stomach. It was warm and weird and wonderful all at the same time and it scratched lightly on the door of my memory until I recalled the last time I'd felt it. It was a sensation that was attributable only to Joe. I allowed the old feelings to return, making me feel beautiful and peaceful and alive. I couldn't help but wonder if the exquisite flood of emotions and sentimentality that was being released inside of me could possibly be construed as an infidelity on my part. Was I being an adulteress? I wondered.

"Would you stop with the guilt please?" I heard Joe say from somewhere above my head and I laughed in spite of myself.

"Listen," I said, jerking my head up to stare into his lovely face again, "there's something I've been dying to ask you."

"Ask away," he invited.

"It's about that wink you gave me ten years ago, do you know the one I'm talking about?"

He took his time and thought for a moment. "You mean that first night you met Jim and you guys took off on his Harley together?"

"Yeah, that's right," I said enthusiastically. "We were stopped at a red light and I was staring at the medal Jim always wore around his neck and the next thing I knew, I saw *you* looking back at me from the medal, remember?"

"I do," Joe said calmly. "I absolutely do remember."

"And you winked at me. Remember that?"

"Yes," he replied. "And your question is . . . ?"

"Well, I always kind of wondered what you really meant by that wink," I said and I noticed that my tone sounded a little meek now. I hate when I get all mushy and unsure of myself like that.

"What did you think I meant?" Joe asked, politely ignoring my sudden fit of self-doubt.

This time I was the one to hesitate before answering. "Well, I took it to mean that you approved, you know? I figured it was your way of telling me that Jim Maguire was the right guy for me. You know, my soul mate and all that. Was I right?"

"Could be," Joe said with a teasing smile.

"Well, I think you might have been wrong," I deadpanned.

He looked surprised at that. "Oh?" was all he said.

Once again, tears welled up in my eyes, demanding release. Ten years worth of doubt, disappointment, and angst over my marriage instantly liquefied and streamed down my cheeks. What came out of my mouth next surprised me as much as it surprised Joe.

"I've fallen out of love with my husband," I blubbered, "and I've prayed to you for the last ten years for some kind of help, but you never even heard me! You weren't listening, were you?"

Joe looked a little hurt at that and I was immediately sorry I'd been so blunt with him. Until precisely this moment, I'd had no idea that I'd been carrying around such a heavy grudge against both Joe and my husband, the two most significant people in my life. But there was no turning back now. I'd said what I'd been too afraid to verbalize for all of this time and there was no way of taking it back. Not that I really wanted to.

"Do you really believe that, Christine?" Joe asked quietly. "After everything I taught you, do you really think I wasn't there for you?" For the first time ever, he didn't wait for an answer from me. "Because I was, you know," he insisted. "I was always there for you but, if you don't mind my saying so, you were usually so busy running the universe, you failed to notice me."

That certainly rang true but I didn't want to get into a long list of my shortcomings yet, so I just stood there sniffling, sniveling, and bawling without saying a word, intelligent or otherwise. I simply wanted to be convinced of his love for me again.

"I was there on your wedding day," Joe went on. "And I know you were aware of me then. Am I right?"

"Okay, that one I remember," I agreed. "I definitely felt your presence that day."

"And I was there when you were in labor with little Joey and again two years later with Gracie," he added.

"It sure didn't feel like it," I pouted. "Those were both times when I definitely didn't think you heard me."

"How could I have missed?" he laughed. "You yelled my name pretty loud as I recall."

I was a little embarrassed at that but, as usual,

I still needed more proof. "Well, okay, I'll give you that one, too," I conceded, "but what about money? What about the fact that I have a bad back, bunions, and chronic fatigue and yet, I still have to go to that wretched job just to make ends meet? What about that, huh?"

Joe remained silent so long that I wondered if I had crossed a line this time. Just as I was about to apologize though, he began rocking me ever so slightly in his strong, loving arms. It amazed me then how quickly I could switch hats and go from being an angry, accusing adult, to a confused and frightened child who needed comforting.

"Your current lifestyle may require you to work at the hospital for right now," he crooned softly into my ear, "but it doesn't require you to be wretched over it."

Of course, he was right but I didn't feel like getting into it with him right now. I had no idea how to go about embracing a job that was slowly eroding all of my altruistic notions, at least what was left of them, and I didn't want a lecture. I was simply too emotionally volatile at the moment to think clearly. I just wanted to be comforted and I was counting on Joe to understand that.

He didn't let me down. Before I could come up with any more accusations of negligence, Joe protectively pulled me close to him again. I leaned my head against his chest and he tugged affectionately on my ponytail, making me feel like a little girl again.

"I thought we straightened this out ten years ago," he sighed, "but I suppose a little reinforcement wouldn't hurt." He hugged me tighter then. "Let me tell you a little bit about what I've witnessed in your life over the past decade," he said, "and then you decide whether or not I've been listening, okay?"

I nodded silently and then I heard his deep, resonant voice echoing from within his chest cavity. He relayed a litany of events, some of which even I would not have been able to accurately recall.

I squirmed when he mentioned that I'd secretly been marking the Scotch bottles for years now as a way of gauging how much alcohol Jim consumed in a night. He told me about the post-partum depression I'd suffered after both births and how I'd kept it a secret from my husband and from my co-workers. He knew about the night I'd put on my coat and walked out the door because the kids were driving me crazy. He recounted how I had simply stood beneath the window and watched them from outside of the house, while crying quietly into the snow-covered hedges. He understood that I had been stretched to a breaking point that night and he even commended me for taking a 'time-out' for myself, rather than saying or doing anything I might have later regretted.

As if that wasn't enough, Joe went on to inform me that I was jealous of my own daughter. I opened my mouth to protest, then stopped because I knew he was right. He said that, though I only wanted the very best in life for Gracie, I also envied the opportunities and choices she would have that had not been available to me. Unlike the generations of women who had preceded her, Gracie's life would be filled with possibilities that were no longer limited by gender.

All of this honesty was giving me a headache, but Joe was relentless. He moved on to the topic of work and talked about how inferior I felt about being simply a 'staff nurse'. He was very much aware that I felt mediocre at best because I didn't work in the Intensive Care Unit or the Operating Room, or some other high-tech branch of nursing that commanded more respect. I didn't even attempt to disagree.

After that, he talked about how I avoided the beach because I couldn't stand looking at myself in a bathing suit anymore. Even worse, he was well aware that I never went down to the club to listen to Jim and his band play anymore because I was afraid that his young and adoring fans would wonder what Jim Maguire ever saw in me; his frumpy, overweight, cranky wife.

Then Joe pulled out the big guns and began to address my marriage. He said that I resented Jim's artistic talent because I was convinced that I had absolutely no such flair of my own. Joe said I begrudged not only Jim's talent, but also the fact that he got such tremendous pleasure from what he did for a living, while I had to put my nose to the grindstone each and every day and muscle my way through my shifts at the hospital.

I marveled at how there was not even the slightest hint of judgment in Joe's tone as he listed these character defects in me. In fact, I sensed nothing but pure love, understanding, and even sympathy flowing from him.

Finally, Joe mentioned one, last resentment that even I had not yet dared to put into words. I winced as I heard him declare that I was afraid the kids loved their father more than they loved me.

That one really got to me. Not only because it was true, but because it was also the most hurtful observation Joe had made so far. My children are the most important thing in the world to me, bar none. Yet, all the time that I spend away from them makes me feel like I'm losing my connection to them. That's what really terrifies me. The simple fact is that, because of our crazy schedules, Jim gets to spend more of the busy, happy, daytime hours with them while I pour all of my energy into the only job that actually supports us. In all fairness though, I have to admit that Jim is usually a lot more fun than I am, and in a better mood too.

I should have known I couldn't hide such painful feelings from Joe. Under great protest from me, he had somehow reached far down into my gut and pulled out each of my darkest secrets. I was astounded to find that sharing all of these hidden, private fears with another person had actually begun to diminish them. Suddenly, I was feeling remarkably better.

Joe had provided a safe environment for me to be honest with myself. He had somehow given a voice to every last one of my resentments and flaws, every irate and unspoken word that was still stuck in my throat, and every dagger that was still embedded in my heart from the angry words Jim and I sometimes exchanged. When he was finished, Joe held me quietly and stroked my hair.

"It's all right," he said. "It's gonna get better, Christine. I promise."

"But it all feels so hopeless," I sobbed from the vicinity of his armpit where I'd kept my head buried. "It's too much, Joe. I've got way too many changes to make. I don't think I'm up to it."

Joe laughed. "Of course you are," he said.

A spark of annoyance ignited into a burning flame in my stomach when he said that. This wasn't funny. I had just been brought to my knees by the immensity of the challenges that lay ahead, and I had almost no confidence that I could right the many wrongs that had been pointed out to me.

"I see we're still a little sensitive," Joe said, soothingly.

"I can't do it, Joe," I stated flatly, finally lifting my head to face him. "I'm still struggling with the same three problems I've struggled with my entire life, only on a larger scale now. My relationships, my job, and my weight are still the three biggest obstacles to my happiness and I just can't seem to conquer them. I don't even know where to begin."

"Maybe conquering them isn't the best approach," he delicately suggested. "Maybe accepting things the way they are is as good a start as any," he continued, "and from there, try to do things that support change."

I pulled away from him then, though I don't really understand why. "Joe, this is all too much for me right now, okay?" I cut in. "I'm tired, I'm emotional, and I have a million things to do in the next couple of hours. I can't just sit around 'accepting things as they are'."

Joe looked wounded for a fleeting moment,

but he recovered quickly. "If you don't mind my saying so," he said politely, "it didn't look like you invested all that much emotion into doing CPR on old Harry in there."

"Weeeell, no," I said slowly, gathering my thoughts for a good defense. "I mean, what do you expect? I'm a professional."

"Oh, right," he said, nodding. "I see."

There was an awkward silence between us then and I didn't know what to say. I knew I had been over-reacting and behaving badly, but I desperately had needed to feel heard and understood, and this had been the first opportunity I'd had to do so in a very long time. It amazed me that no matter how testy I got with him, Joe never took offense. I wished I could be like that.

I knew I had to get home to wake the kids for soccer practice and get breakfast started, but I didn't want to leave things on a sour note like this. I guess Joe must have heard my thoughts again because he gently took the keys from my hand and opened the car door for me.

"Hey, do you still have that little gold charm I gave you?" he asked, brightening. "You know, the one with your six guidelines on it?"

My heart sank. "No," I admitted. "I'm afraid I don't. Gracie flushed it down the toilet by accident when she was two."

He didn't look the least bit upset by this turn

of events. "Do you, by any chance, remember what number three was?" he asked, and I wasn't sure if this was a trick question or a sincere request.

"Number three?" I said, stalling. "Um, was that the one about dropping the ego or something?"

"Nope," he said shaking his head. Suddenly, he seemed a lot more chipper now that he was tormenting me with riddles the way he used to do in the old days.

I grinned sheepishly. "Well, don't keep me in suspense," I goaded him.

"Take care of yourself first and foremost," he declared. "That's what it says."

I waited for a further explanation, which experience had taught me could not be too far behind. What he said next though, knocked the wind out of me.

"Don't you see, Christine?" Joe said with palpable sincerity. "You haven't fallen out of love with your husband; you've fallen out of love with *yourself.*"

Those words landed on my heart with the weight of a wrecking ball, smashing to smithereens all of my previous notions about my failing marriage. Could that be true? Was there still hope for saving my marriage? And, more importantly, did I alone hold the key?

I blinked my eyes and reluctantly came back

to the present moment. Joe was holding the car door open and guiding me inside now. Trance-like, I dropped into the driver's seat as though I had not one bone in my entire body.

In slow motion, I put the key in the ignition and Joe leaned inside the open window. "Fall in love with yourself again, Christine," he whispered, "and you'll see everything shift back into its proper place. And I do mean *everything*."

The next thing I knew, I found myself pulling out of the parking lot and heading for home in an altered state. A breathy and prolonged, "Wow," was the only response I was able to muster as the car moved east toward the rising, August sun.

FOUR

Jim and the kids were already up when I walked through the door. They were all seated at the breakfast table in various stages of their meals. Joey and Gracie were each dressed in blue and white uniforms with the words, 'Neptune City Soccer League' etched in big blue letters across the front of their shirts and the name 'MaGuire' sewn neatly across each of their little backsides. Jim, his eyes still puffy from sleep, or maybe too many drinks last night, was pouring orange juice and handing out napkins with practiced efficiency.

I watched him from the doorway for a moment and wondered why I cared how much he'd had to drink last night. It's not like his alcohol consumption affected my life at all. He's the one who has to suffer the hangover, I told myself. Still, I wondered how many he'd had and, more importantly, with whom he'd had them.

Joey was the first to notice my somewhat dazed entrance. "Hi, Mom," he called through a mouthful of Cheerios. "Did you remember to get Pop Tarts?"

"What? Pop Tarts?" I answered dully. "I think so. Why don't you go out to the car and bring in some of the packages, sweetie, okay?"

"Well, I hope you remembered the red licorice," Gracie chimed in. "You promised, remember?"

I felt Jim staring at me. "You okay, Christine? You look a little . . . funny."

"Oh, yeah. Yeah, I'm fine," I lied. "I . . . um . . . I'm sorry I'm so late."

I was not about to discuss my encounter with Joe simply because it was just too personal. My mind raced as I tried to think of a believable explanation for my tardiness. If worse came to worst, I figured I could always use the CPR story. It wouldn't exactly be a lie, just what the nuns used to refer to as 'a sin of omission'.

Jim looked confused. "You're not late, Chris," he said. "You're right on schedule."

I looked at the clock and, sure enough, it was only six-fifteen, my usual hour of arrival. That meant I still had time to take a shower and get to work by seven. What was going on? The conversation with Joe had to have lasted at least twenty or thirty minutes, I thought, and I distinctly remembered looking at the clock in the check out line and noting that it was exactly ten after six. How could the time I'd spent with Joe have not existed?

"You sure you're okay?" Jim was asking. "You seem . . . different."

"I'm just tired," I answered out of habit.

Jim expertly caught a bagel in mid-air as it popped out of the toaster. "So, what else is new," he mumbled under his breath, and it wasn't a question.

I readied myself to come back at him with a snide comment of my own. I began putting together phrases in my mind about how hard I worked, how little I slept, and how I was entitled to be tired, when suddenly, I realized something absolutely amazing; I wasn't tired at all! For maybe the first time since Joey was born nine years ago, I didn't feel utterly exhausted. In fact, I felt pretty good. No, *great*—I felt great, energetic, and maybe even a little exhilarated! What was happening to me? This wasn't normal.

I dashed headlong toward the bathroom, leaving Jim dazed and confused in my wake. I flipped on the bright, overhead light on the ceiling, and stared into the mirror. What I saw there shocked me.

Christine Moore stared back at me, her face dewy, peaceful, and unlined even under the harsh 120-watt indoor floodlight. Next, the chronic ache in my lower back mysteriously vanished into thin air, as did the dull pain in my bunions.

There was no doubt in my mind that Joe had something to do with this.

Like forbidden lovers who press their hands against opposite sides of the prison glass that separates them, I placed my forty-eight year old fingertips delicately against the lovely image of my younger self on the other side of the mirror. My reflection's hands were alabaster and smooth with the plumpness of youth when she lifted them toward me. The hands on my side of the mirror, though, were webbed with tiny dry lines and skin transparent enough to reveal the prominent knuckles and blue veins beneath. Mesmerized, I leaned in for an even closer look.

"Where did you go?" I whispered, leaving a thin mist of breath on the glass.

"Christine?" I heard Jim call from the hallway. "Are you all right?"

Before I could answer, he was standing in the doorway and the lovely figure in the mirror vanished just as quickly as she had appeared.

"Actually, I'm fine," I answered, "I've never been better."

Worriedly, Jim looked me over from head to

toe, then shook his head. I don't think he believed me.

The entire time I showered, I thought about the events of the morning and about my conversation with Joe. Though I fiercely resisted it, the subtle beginnings of hope and optimism were trying to take root inside my heart once again. I loved the feeling, but didn't dare to trust it. I was afraid to believe that things might possibly get better, but I was even more afraid to think that they wouldn't.

There was so much I had forgotten to ask Joe while I'd had the chance, and now I regretted the oversights. For instance, I wondered if he still rode a Harley. I hadn't seen him arrive or leave, so I didn't know for certain, but I hoped he still did. There was something about the idea of him on that magnificent machine that exuded freedom, authenticity, and power over oneself . . . all things that Joe stood for.

Mostly, though, I regretted not asking how I could contact him or when I would see him again, if ever. I wondered if Joe would call me at home, then I immediately worried that he might. What would Jim think if he answered the phone? What would Joe say to him? What would I say to him? And why was I so racked with guilt if I wasn't doing anything wrong?

An entire week went by without an

appearance or a word from Joe. Even so, I found evidence of burgeoning miracles in places I never would have thought to look. For instance, my sweet tooth began to disappear. When I watched Gracie sitting in front of the television devouring her red licorice, I wasn't the least bit tempted to take a few strands for myself. Truth be told, I actually found the stuff repulsive, which is odd because it used to be one of my very favorite treats.

Then, by sheer accident, I came across the old, gold-plated name pin I'd purchased right after graduation from nursing school. I considered that to be another little miracle of sorts, since I didn't even know I still had it. I discovered it buried beneath some old, junk-jewelry I had been sorting through for Gracie and her friends to play with. I hadn't seen it in at least fifteen years and now, nostalgically, I nestled the coveted pin in my hand and read the tarnished inscription. 'Christine Moore, R.N.' it said, and I remembered how proud I once had been to add those initials to my name.

Policies and procedures had changed drastically at Valley Community Hospital since those days and probably everywhere else as well. Nowadays, registered nurses at our hospital were required to wear the same, corporate-issued, laminated tags that everyone else did, including x-ray technicians, orderlies, and even the housekeeping department. The tag contained the hospital logo with a photo I.D. that listed the employee's first name only, followed by a short slogan that read 'Partners in Care'. Nowhere on the tag was there any mention of the person's title or status. No matter what level of education or degree of technical ability one had attained, we had all been neatly homogenized into 'partners in care'.

This tended to give the patients a false sense of security, I thought, and made it easy for them to wrongly assume that everyone who participated in their care was a registered nurse. How convenient for Valley Community Hospital.

I promptly dropped the tarnished, old name pin into a jar of jewelry cleaner, then rubbed it with a soft cloth until it sparkled. The next day at work, I did something completely out of character for me. I boldly wore the shiny, gold nameplate, advertising my 'R.N.' along with an 'I dare you to say anything' attitude. The amazing thing was that no one, not even the anal-retentive administrative assistant on my floor, challenged me on it. Yet, another small miracle.

In the aftermath of my meeting with Joe, I have to admit that I began finding reasons to go to the Shop-Well more than was absolutely necessary. I told myself that we needed milk, and then deliberately forgot to buy cereal while I was there. Back I went the following morning. Even though I only picked up one or two items at a time, I went down each and every aisle on a sort of reconnaissance mission, hoping to stumble upon Joe again.

Jim grew more and more concerned about what he perceived as an alarming amount of absentmindedness on my part lately. Though he clearly was impressed by all the extra energy I suddenly had, I noticed the scrutinizing stares and odd looks he tossed in my direction each time I announced yet another trip to the grocery store.

I also began sprucing up a little in the mornings before I left for the Shop-Well. Not that I put all that much effort into it, but I took the time to put on a minimal amount of makeup and to brush my hair before pulling it into a ponytail. A couple of times I noticed Jim sniffing the air in his sleep after I dabbed on a few drops of perfume and I had to smile. I also began tying a colorful scarf around my ponytail instead of just letting the covered elastic do its job. Well, Joe had mentioned something about taking better care of myself, hadn't he? Besides, how was I supposed to fall in love with myself again if I went out in public looking like I'd just rolled out of bed?

After the second futile week of scouring the

aisles of Shop-Well for even a trace of Joe, I began to realize how foolishly I was behaving. From past experience I knew that if Joe wanted to make his presence known, he would have no problem tracking me down.

Another week passed and I was beginning to have so much energy that I actually began wearing my running shoes to the store so that I could squeeze in a morning jog along the beach after I got the groceries. I hadn't run in years and I was embarrassed to be seen doing so along the boardwalk where all the really serious runners did their morning work-out routines. I figured I wouldn't humiliate myself too badly if I avoided the boardwalk altogether, at least until I got into a little better shape.

I decided to run along the hard-packed sand down by the water where hardly anyone runs for fear of ruining expensive running shoes in the salty, swirling tide. My shoes could sustain no further damage anyway since I'd cut a slit in each of them to make room for my protruding bunions. It was the only way I could manage to run without unbearable pain. I'd never had to go through antics like this when I was young, I realized, but then I hadn't been so sadly out of shape either.

I commenced my new routine by stretching as much as my near-comatose muscles would allow. I stood by the water's edge and twisted and turned in every direction as far as my stiff joints would permit. At long last, I was ready.

The morning was soft with a sky the color of pink lemonade. I took a deep breath and broke into an easy jog. A cool mist wafted off the tops of the cresting waves and spritzed me with a refreshing dampness. I began to feel more and more awake with each breath of pristine, ocean air that filled my stagnant lungs. I'd decided not to measure any kind of distance but to just keep my eye on the time and try to run consistently for twenty minutes.

That turned out to be a lot harder than I had expected. After only the first five minutes, I was uncomfortably aware of certain muscle groups that hadn't felt life in more than a decade. Perspiration dampened my forehead and a side-stitch made its presence known. Undaunted, I pressed on.

Another lone runner passed me from the opposite direction and nodded acknowledgement as he went by. I managed to slow my breathing enough to give the erroneous impression that I wasn't in any discomfort. Of course, the minute he was out of earshot, I slowed down and let out an agonized groan.

When twenty minutes had finally passed, I came to an abrupt halt and began walking in small circles, hands on my hips, panting and sweating profusely now. I stopped and then bent forward, trying to catch my breath and ease the pain in my side.

I was completely unaware of the longhaired man seated on a Harley Davidson only a few feet away in the sand.

"Suffering is not a requirement for losing weight," said a melodious voice.

Though the tone was genial, it startled me out of my self-absorption and I jerked to attention. "Joe," I exhaled, awestruck by the sight of him.

I gulped in some much needed air, unsure if I was breathless from the exercise or from the thrill of seeing him again. As though through the lens of a special camera, I saw Joe in soft focus this time, his face as radiant as the shimmering sea and his features softly lit by the pink glow of the morning sky.

"What do you think of that sunrise?" he asked, gesturing with his eyes toward the luminescent sky behind me.

I turned and looked upward. I took in the lustrous pink hues of the heavens as well as a bright crimson border that was now lighting up the horizon, like a warm-up act for the emerging sun. "It's just beautiful," I sighed. "Truly magnificent."

"So are you, Christine," was all he said.

"Excuse me?"

"That's exactly what you're like," he added

after a slight pause. "Don't rush this fitness thing or anything else for that matter. You're beautiful at every stage, Christine . . . just like a sunrise. Try to enjoy the process."

Hot tears stung my eyes. It had to have been years since a man had thought me beautiful and until that precise moment, I did not know how very much I had longed to hear those words again.

This time I didn't stop to think. I ran to Joe and threw my grateful arms around his neck as he engulfed me in a warm and loving embrace. "Things aren't as hard as you try to make them seem, Christine," he whispered close to my ear. "It's all so much easier than you want to believe it is."

"Okay, I'll try to remember that," I promised, lifting my face to stare into his mahogany eyes. "It's just that I get overwhelmed so easily, you know? I worry about the kids and money and Jim and me and what's going to happen if we don't get it together pretty soon with our relationship and . . ."

Joe pressed his finger against the hollow above my upper lip. "Shhhhh," he said, smiling. "Let me give you an easy way of knowing what your top priority is each day, okay? Ready?"

"Tell me," I gulped.

"Look in the mirror," he said. "Really. It's that simple." Joe cupped my face in his hands as he spoke. "If you want to know what your job is, look into the mirror and whatever you see staring back at you is what I want you to take especially good care of that day."

"But I'll always see the same thing," I protested, "me."

"Precisely," he said.

"But . . ."

"But that's the whole point," he continued. "If I wanted you to count how many drinks Jim had last night or with whom he was drinking, you would see Jim's face looking back at you in the mirror. But you don't, do you? Because taking care of Jim is Jim's business and taking care of you is yours. Got that?"

"But . . ."

"But nothing." Joe laughed then. "Why is it the simplest lessons are always the hardest for you to accept? I gave you *this* body and *this* life to do with as you please, but I did not give you anyone else's life to control. Does that make sense to you?"

I didn't say anything right away. I mean, Joe was right, of course. It's just that I didn't see how things were going to get done if I didn't stay alert and in control of the financial and practical aspects of taking care of the family.

"And by the way," he added with a mischievous grin, "Running the universe is my job, not yours, okay? We clear on that?"

I was scared. Joe seemed to be suggesting that I give up control over all the things he seemed to think I had no control over anyway. He was hinting that my sense of power and efficiency were just illusions, I supposed. But I couldn't stop wondering what would happen if I left everything to chance. How would the housework get done? Who would make lunch for the kids? Where would the groceries come from and, more importantly, where would the money for these things come from?

No, I decided, Joe was definitely wrong on this one. Someone had to take responsibility for running a household and that someone had to be me. The indisputable truth is that my husband is a dreamer and an artist, while I am practical, sensible, and a realist. I know how to take control of a situation and more than twenty years in the nursing profession had proved that. There was no doubt in my mind that I had to be the one to take charge here. I opened my mouth to say so, but Joe was already speaking.

"Where is the romance in your life, Christine?" he asked, and the question surprised me. "And while we're on the subject, where's your sense of humor? Your creativity? Your sense of fun? Your passion?"

I was vaguely aware that my mouth was hanging open, but oddly enough, no words were forthcoming.

Joe pointed at the horizon behind me. "Look," he murmured softly.

Obediently, I turned and what I witnessed made me gasp with awe and wonder. The sky was an indescribable mixture of pink and gold hues, silhouetting graceful sailboats that glided by in the distance. A burst of wispy, flame-colored clouds escorted the majestic golden sun above the ocean's edge now, spilling a soft flaxen light across the beach.

"Oh, Joe," I breathed, unable to take my eyes away from the spectacular sight in front of me. "You're so right. Where is the romance in my life?"

I waited for his knowing reply. When it didn't come, I turned and, except for a fresh set of motorcycle tire tracks, I was shocked to see that the beach was completely empty.

FIVE

Joe's questions haunted me over the next few days. I couldn't stop wondering how one went about rediscovering qualities that were as intangible as romance, fun, passion, and creativity. Where did he even expect me to begin? Besides, any reasonable person over the age of forty knows that those traits are usually long gone by middle age. If I had to guess, I'd say I'd lost them in the same mysterious dark caverns of my mind that had also swallowed up my enthusiasm, idealism, and hope for a bright future.

Survival and financial security had insidiously replaced the frivolous goals of youth and maybe that's the way it's supposed to be. I mean, by the time you have a family, you have a lot more to worry about than your own passions and good times. At least, that's what I'd always believed. If this was Joe's usual, roundabout way of pointing me in a new direction, I figured he might as well ask me to pull a rabbit out of a hat. I simply couldn't do it.

I sat in the car thinking about all of this while I was parked outside of the karate studio, waiting for the kids to finish their twice-weekly lesson. I planned to shuttle them home for a quick dinner, get Joey started on his homework, then drop Gracie off at her ballet class. That's when an odd thing occurred. Joey burst out of the studio doors and into the car, carrying a small carton filled with grass and bits of lettuce. Before I could ask any questions, Gracie followed on his heels cuddling a small, scrawny rabbit in the shelter of her plump little arms.

I guess I shouldn't have been surprised.

"Mom!" Joey bellowed with the excitement known only to nine year olds, "Gracie found a rabbit! Can we keep him? Please, Mom, please? He won't be any trouble. Can we? Please?"

"You don't know he's a 'he'," Gracie taunted her brother. "He might be a girl, right, Mom?" she said holding the trembling animal close to her heart. "Can we keep her, Mommy? Please, can we? I already named her 'Jersey'."

That's when another odd thing happened. I heard myself saying 'yes' in spite of the fact that I knew I would be the one who would ultimately end up taking care of the sickly, little animal. I had no conscious idea at the time that the semi-starving rabbit in my daughter's lap would act as a catalyst for some remarkable changes in the dynamics of our family.

Gracie decided that she didn't want to go to her ballet lesson that night and, though I knew I should have given her a lecture on responsibility and finishing what you start, the truth is that I was relieved. I didn't feel like driving any more today, not to mention that it gave me the opportunity to cook some of the fresh vegetables and pasta I'd bought earlier this morning on one of my daily excursions to the Shop-Well.

I never dreamed I'd ever look forward to cooking, but strangely enough, now that I had some unexpected time on my hands, I was suddenly eager to create a real, home-cooked and unhurried meal for my children. Jim had a couple of tutoring sessions lined up at the elementary school in Bradley Beach and then a gig with his band later on at *Harold's Pub*, so he wouldn't be home until much later tonight. For some reason, I felt relieved about that too. I guess I felt a little freer to experiment with my cooking, not that Jim had ever criticized it. I guess I was just always afraid that he might.

I actually found myself humming as I boiled the water for pasta and began chopping

tomatoes, scallions, and fresh garlic. Then I
noticed a very odd sound coming from the living
room where Joey and Gracie were playing with
their new pet. It was the peculiar and marvelous
sound of conversation. Unbelievably, in their
childlike zest for 'Jersey', they had foregone the
usual distractions of television, video games, and
CD players. For once, there was no other noise
overriding the giggles and the excited banter of
my two children. Their laughter and squeals of
delight tickled my ears and momentarily I
stopped all the chopping and listened to them
with a great big smile growing inside of my heart.

We ate dinner at the table—together—
without watching the clock and without the
television blaring in the background. I am
embarrassed to admit that I don't even remember
the last time we did that. The kids recounted
how Grace had spotted the rabbit on the school
lawn, how Joey had helped her to catch it, and
how Gracie's teacher had discussed with them
the finer points of rabbit cuisine. We laughed,
we talked, we ate and I was vaguely aware that
some starving corner of my soul was, at long
last, being fed.

I cleaned up the dishes and watched through
the kitchen window as Gracie and Joey played a
lighthearted game of tag in the yard. The
September evening was still warm and gentle in
the fading last days of summer. Even the once

irritating sound of the screen door slamming now brought pleasant memories to mind of my own carefree days of childhood and I was acutely aware that I had just been handed a precious gift.

The kids settled down and did their homework at the kitchen table while I made sandwiches for their lunches. I busied myself with the jar of peanut butter and Joey asked if I'd like to take an 'intelligence quiz'. I agreed and he read some simple questions to me while I casually answered amid the fruit, bread, jars, and plastic wrap. Gracie and Joey both giggled at my answers and I had no idea what was so funny until Joey got a mischievous look on his face after the tenth question and said, "Thanks for doin' my homework, Mom."

For whatever reason, I refrained from giving a lecture on honesty and instead, laughed at myself. To my surprise, laughing felt much better than lecturing.

After their baths, we all convened in Gracie's room while they got into their pajamas and prepared for bed. They both wanted to sleep with the rabbit tonight and it was decided that Joey would sleep in the extra twin bed in Gracie's room so the rabbit 'wouldn't get lonely'. The kids each kissed me goodnight, then ran over to the carton in the corner of the room and said goodnight to Jersey.

"Mommy?" Joey called as I left the room. I hadn't heard him call me that in a very long time. Usually, it's 'Mom' or 'Ma'—never 'Mommy'.

"What is it, honey?" I said from the doorway.

"I had fun tonight."

"Me, too." I smiled.

"Me, too," Gracie piped up from her bed.

Joey wasn't done though. "Do you think if Gracie quit ballet and we both quit karate, we could do this all the time?" he asked. "I'd much rather be with you than my karate teacher."

"Me, too," Gracie echoed.

I was glad it was dark so my children wouldn't see the maelstrom of tears that erupted in my heart and spilled past the barrier of my blinking eyes. I retraced my steps and sat on the side of Joey's bed in the dark. I cradled him in my arms and kissed his cool, smooth cheek. "That sounds like a nice idea," I said, hoping my voice did not reflect the overwhelming emotions that were consuming me. I got up and kissed Gracie next. "In fact, that sounds like a wonderful idea. Let's talk about it in the morning, okay?"

After the children were asleep, I stepped outside, dragging my ancient, rusty beach chair onto the lawn. I plopped down into it and stared up at the night sky, inhaling the last of the floral-scented, summer atmosphere. Raising my face to the stars, I began searching for the constellations I had memorized as a child. I had barely spotted the Big Dipper when I became aware of a warm hand covering mine as I rested it on the arm of my beach chair. I should have been scared, but I wasn't. I knew who it was.

"You were wonderful tonight," Joe said quietly.

"Thanks," I murmured, still staring at Polaris.

"Happy?" he asked.

"Funny you should ask," I answered with a smirk. "I feel happier now than I have in years. I'm not sure I understand it, but I'm not fighting it either. I'm just enjoying it."

"Good."

That's when I realized how unusual it was for me to accept happiness where I could find it. Usually I looked for it in the bottom of a quart of ice cream, or on my annual job review, or on the scale, or in my paycheck. Now, I realized that I was feeling very fulfilled for no particular reason. Normally at this hour, I would be exhausted and raid the refrigerator for some comfort or energy or a thousand other things. For the first time since I could remember, I wasn't hungry now. A little herbal tea would be nice, I thought, but that's about all I really wanted.

"I'm glad you're back in communication with your body," Joe said matter-of-factly. "That's always a good place to be."

Magically, a forty-eight year old curtain of

confusion began to lift. It dawned on me then that I'd been living mostly in my head and almost never in my body. I treated my physical being as if it had no right to an opinion or a voice. No wonder I had struggled for so long over my weight. I was always telling myself what to eat and never listening to what my body had to say.

"Can it really be that simple, Joe?" I asked with noticeable trepidation. "I never stop to check in with how I feel. I mean, how I *really* feel. I'm always turning to diets and the so-called experts to tell me what my body needs. But it's not their body, it's mine. I just haven't been listening to it, right?"

"Raise the flag."

I was on a roll and I couldn't stop blabbering. "Tonight I let myself experience feelings that I haven't felt in years and suddenly, I'm not the least bit hungry! This is a real breakthrough, you know that? Help me to remember this, okay? I never want to be separated from my body again!"

Though I knew he was happy for me, Joe remained pensive.

"Are you ready to go deeper?" he finally asked.

"Yeah, sure. Okay." I was lying. One breakthrough a day is more than enough for me, but there was an aura of sadness surrounding Joe tonight and I wanted him to be as happy as I was. Teaching me agonizing lessons seemed to be the only thing that cheered him up when he got like this, so I really didn't mind volunteering for some more insight.

"Have you thought about our last conversation?" he wanted to know. "The one about romance and fun and creativity?"

"Of course, I did," I answered proudly. "Didn't you see me tonight? Didn't you see that pasta dish I made? Talk about creativity!"

Joe wasn't laughing though, and that frightened me. "Let's talk about your relationship with Jim," he suggested. "How's that going?"

"It's okay, I guess," I said tentatively. "I mean, I don't get to see him all that much, so, yeah, it's all right I suppose."

Joe squeezed my hand then and leaned forward to face me this time. There was an intensity, an urgency about him that I'd never seen before. "'All right' isn't good enough, Christine," he said. "You've got to demand more of yourself in the way of your relationships. You've got to light the fire again. You've got to get the feelings back. Do you understand?"

I didn't like that all the responsibility for the health of our marriage seemed to be landing on my shoulders. I mean, I'm willing to admit that maybe some of the blame belongs to me and maybe I've made some mistakes, but so has Jim. It does take two people to have any kind of a relationship after all. Why was Joe putting the entire burden on me? I certainly hoped he wasn't about to tell me that I wasn't trying hard enough because if he was, he was in for an argument. I did the lion's share of the work around the house, not to mention making most of the money, while Jim sat in a bar drinking and playing music. Oh, no. I was not about to give in on this point.

"No, Joe," I said evenly, "I *don't* understand. It takes more than one person to put the spark back into a relationship," I said. "I can't do it alone, you know."

"You're wrong, Christine." He corrected me without any trace of judgment in his voice. "In order to have romance with your partner, you have to first be a romantic yourself. You have to be capable of living the romantic life all by yourself."

I was stunned. "I do?"

"You have to reach deep down inside of yourself and find your sense of adventure, remember how to have fun again, ignite your passions. That's what romance is really all about. It has very little to do with the other person in your life and everything to do with how you see yourself. If you forget what real romance is, just watch your children because they are all romantics. They can show you how to revel in each and every moment if you watch them carefully enough."

A terrible thought struck me then. "Are you getting ready to leave me again, Joe?" I asked as gently as I've ever asked anything. "Because I'm not ready yet. I have no idea how to put my life back together again. I still need you, Joe."

"I understand," he said. "I'm not leaving any time soon. It's just that I really want you . . . and the rest of the world . . . to get this love thing right."

I breathed a sigh of relief. At least I was assured of a temporary reprieve. "I'm trying, Joe," I insisted. "I'll try even harder if you want. Just give me a little more direction, okay?"

He brightened at that. "Good. Okay. Tell me, what's the first thing that attracted you to Jim? Be really honest, Christine."

"That's easy," I replied. "His music. I loved what he could do with that saxophone."

"What else?" He pressed me for details. "Try to remember."

"Well, I loved the thought of being in love with a musician," I sheepishly admitted and immediately I felt embarrassed for being so shallow. "It was exciting, you know? I felt like other girls really envied me. I mean, Jim could have had just about anyone he wanted, but he chose me and that made me feel really special."

"Everyone wants to feel special," Joe said gently. "But tell me more about why you fell in love with him."

I wasn't sure what Joe was getting at, but I knew he was always after the truth even when it sounded dumb. With that in mind, I continued. "I saw Jim give half of his sandwich to a homeless man once when he thought I wasn't looking," I finally recalled. "That really touched me."

"I remember," Joe said with a smile. "That touched me too."

"... And he was one of the happiest people I ever met," I added. "I mean, he used to wake up and start singing and whistling first thing in the morning. How many people do you know who do that?" I hesitated for a minute and thought about that. Then I realized that I hadn't heard Jim's familiar whistle or carefree singing in a very long time and suddenly, I was overwhelmed with sadness.

Joe picked up on my cue and switched gears then. "Now, tell me what went wrong," he urged. "Where did all of that love go?" he asked. "And just what is it that you're so afraid of?"

I really didn't want to do this. It hurt to put myself under this cosmic microscope that Joe always wanted to look through. I was just about to deny his request, but when I looked into his sincere and searching eyes, I also knew I didn't want to let him down.

"Power," I admitted weakly. "I'm afraid of giving Jim any power over me."

"Because?"

"Because then he would have everything," I said. "And I'd be at his mercy."

"Oh, Sweetheart," Joe whispered. "Why are you still so afraid to be vulnerable? Why are you still so intimidated by that soft, feminine side of yourself?"

"What?" I said, incredulous. "I'm not afraid of my femininity," I stubbornly insisted. "I'm afraid of being taken advantage of . . . by a man . . . by someone that I love."

Joe shook his head and cast his eyes up toward the stars. He stared in silence while I struggled wordlessly with my own thoughts. I had the strangest sensation then that Joe and I were locked in a silent and invisible war of some sort.

After what seemed like a very long time, Joe finally spoke and his tone was as warm and subdued as the late summer night itself. "The only reason you're afraid of letting Jim get close to you is because you're afraid that he'll be disappointed by what he finds . . . because you're a little disappointed in yourself. Isn't that right, Christine?"

My immediate instinct was to protest but I knew that I would do so in vain. Even as he spoke the words, I knew they were accurate. I hadn't ever wanted Jim to discover that I was just a drone. I saw myself merely as a laborer, working only in the shadow of the spotlight, never quite talented enough to shine on my own. I'd faced the fact long ago that in a world of sleek and glistening racehorses, I was a pack-mule and that's all I would ever be. Who could blame me for not being eager to share that information with my husband?

Joe reached for my hands and folded them both inside of his. "You're an artist of the oldest and most noble lineage, Christine," he said softly. "Do you know that?"

"I am?" I breathed. "How do you figure?"

"You're not a drone," he said, "you're a healer." I cocked my head like an eager puppy and waited for him to continue. "It's your destiny to nurture and to heal, no matter what you choose to do for a living," he said. "People of your ilk used to be called shamans and they were once among the most revered people in society. You're a direct descendent of that line. Obviously, that's why you chose to be a nurse. But modern medicine no longer goes in a direction that supports your talents or fine instincts in that area. That's why it's up to you to find a new path where your light can finally shine."

I was flabbergasted. Speechless. And flattered beyond description.

"You know what else?" he said.

Incapable of a reply, I simply shook my head.

"Everyone on earth is an artist or a performer of sorts," he went on, "but not everyone sees it quite that way. Jim is lucky. He's the kind of artist that is popularly recognized as such. It's much harder for Firefighters and mothers, scientists and waitresses, teachers and accountants to see themselves as the performers that they are. The trick is to find a way of expressing yourself through the work that you do. You need to discover purpose and beauty in all the little things you create throughout the day, whether it's a gourmet pasta dish or a well orchestrated rescue operation, a note of music or a harmonious home, a beautiful painting or a game of tag with your children. It all improves the quality of lives."

By the time I went inside to go to bed that night, I was still dazed by Joe's heartfelt words and thoughts. I felt like I was floating as I looked in on the children and then lightly kissed each of their satin cheeks without waking them.

Before retiring to my own bed, I was drawn to the kitchen once more where I found myself doing something I hadn't done in years. I retrieved my beautiful pasta dish from the refrigerator and set it beside the microwave oven. I then went to the china cabinet, pulled out one of my favorite, hand-painted dishes that I almost never use, and set a place for one at the kitchen table. Lastly, I wrote a few words to Jim on a pink 'post-it' note. It read:

If you're hungry, this piece of my art
is for you.
C.

I stirred slightly in my sleep when Jim returned home from his gig at *Harold's Pub*. Too tired to open my eyes, I was only vaguely aware of the comforting sound of the microwave beeping and the muffled clatter of silverware far off in the distance.

And then my husband tiptoed into our room, slid into bed beside me, and tenderly kissed my bare shoulder. Without warning, I tumbled off a cliff—just like I had ten years ago—and fell into the slumbering memories of our long ago love for one another.

SIX

In addition to the deepening connection with my children, I also began spending more quality time with my patients. After all, I was an artist and when I was at work, the bedside was my canvas. I initiated conversations and discovered that the elderly had fascinating tales to tell if only one could afford the time to listen. In the bottom-line-business of Valley Community Hospital, I certainly couldn't afford the time, but I listened anyway. Instead of doing my paperwork in the sterile silence of the nurse's station, I brought my charts into the patients' rooms, seated myself in a comfortable chair, and encouraged them to speak as I wrote my notes for the shift, occasionally looking up long enough to share a smile with them.

I began to feel like a nurse again. No, a shaman. I loved that term and half-heartedly considered having it put on my nametag. My disposition was improving with each passing day, that is, until I was pulled aside by our clock-watching, number-crunching administrative assistant. He told me that I was spending far too much time at the bedside instead of tending to the important things like charging for supplies and documenting procedures so that the insurance companies would pay us.

I laughed.

He didn't.

"In my opinion, comforting and nurturing the patient is what nursing is all about," I stated flatly, amazed that this non-medical person thought himself in a position to criticize my decades of experience and time-management skills. Unfortunately, he was. The current health care system at Valley Community Hospital granted him that grossly undeserved privilege and there was nothing I could do about it. Or was there?

"Hand-holding does not qualify for third party reimbursement," he informed me without the slightest clue as to how foolish he sounded. "You're a highly paid RN," he continued. "You should have better things to do."

"You're right," I said. "I do. There's a woman

down the hall who just had her hip replaced and who is scared to death to move. She needs someone to reassure her and maybe even to draw a diagram so she can start trusting this new joint in her body." I stood to leave then. "If you'll excuse me, I have *people*, not paperwork, to take care of."

I turned on my heel and went back to my patients then, figuring I had nothing to lose at this point, except a job that I hated doing the way the powers-that-be insisted that I do it. I was certain now that Joe was right about me being an artist and a shaman, and I was not about to turn my back on that. I decided I would do my job the way I knew it should be done and let the chips fall where they may. I was a healer, not a paper-shuffler, and I found tremendous satisfaction in that thought.

I realized then that I had slipped into accepting mediocrity not only in the way I did my job, but also in the way I participated in my marriage. As long as I was being honest, I knew I had to take a closer look at what was going on between Jim and me. In the rare moments when I'd shared my marital woes with other women, the one thing that always came back to me was some nonsense about being grateful for companionship at this age. Why do people always say that? As if having good company is all you can ask for in a relationship after the age of forty. Well, I wanted more. I wanted love and lust and excitement and romance, not this silly thing called companionship. I had numbed my emotions by staying impossibly busy over the years while all other facets of my life had quietly slipped into neutral. I had no intention of operating in that kind of limbo for even one more minute. It was time to shake things up, I decided.

I finished my shift and walked outside into a warm and soft September afternoon. It had rained earlier, but now the sun was shining and there was just the slightest hint of autumn in the clear, crisp skies overhead. As I headed through the crowded parking lot toward my car, I was filled with thoughts and questions about how I could turn things around in my life. I sensed that already some significant changes had begun to take place, especially since I was beginning to feel closer to my kids, and I wondered if maybe I should just be satisfied with that.

"Complacency is never the goal," a familiar voice said, and I wasn't a bit surprised to see Joe sitting on his Harley parked beside my Toyota.

"What's everybody got against comfort zones?" I said laughingly. "If you ask me, they've gotten a bum rap lately."

"Just as long as you remember to keep growing while you're so busy being comfortable," he quipped. He patted the leather seat behind him. "C'mon, take a little joyride with me," Joe invited.

I wasn't expecting that and I got a bit flustered. "What? Oh, no, Joe, I can't."

"Yes, you can," he said with a mischievous grin. "Jim's picking the kids up at school today and, if you don't mind my saying so, you have enough groceries on hand to feed a small army."

"But . . ."

"But unless you have something better to do than figure out the meaning of life," he said, "I'd say this was as good a time as any for some serious soul-searching." He bit the curve of his lower lip to subdue a teasing smile and waited for my answer.

A little self-consciously, I reached for the extra helmet he was holding out to me and climbed aboard.

We pulled out of the hospital parking lot amid the stares and startled glances of flower-carrying visitors and employees who were changing shifts. I suppose I shouldn't have been surprised by their reactions. In the somewhat dignified and conservative medical community, Joe and I did make an unlikely pair: a middle-aged nurse dressed in hospital scrubs, taking off on a motorcycle with a longhaired, wild-looking guy who nods his head and smiles at everyone they pass. The funny thing is, I rather enjoyed it.

We picked up a little speed and headed north
on Ocean Avenue as the briny scent of the sea
washed over my face. I exhaled the stale hospital
air and sucked in a lung full of fresh, pristine
ocean mist as we sped past houses, hot dog stands,
and restaurants. "Where are we going?" I yelled
into Joe's ear.

"Sandy Hook," he called back over the
engine's roar.

Sandy Hook is a tiny peninsula off the Jersey
shore that reaches out into the ocean in the form
of a hook, hence the name. The beaches there
are undeveloped and beautiful in a rugged way
and when the sky is clear, as it often is in the
early fall, you can see across the water to
Manhattan.

Joe drove a few miles to the farthest end of
the hook and pulled into the last available
parking lot. We dismounted and hung our
helmets on the handlebars like a couple of
seasoned bikers. I removed my shoes then, and
carried them in my hand as we made our way
toward the water.

I stole a glance at Joe while we walked and I
was caught off guard by how physically attractive
he was. The ocean breeze rippled through his
long locks of hair and the sun bounced off the
silver flecks that were scattered throughout.
Though Joe was not magazine-cover-handsome,
there was a look of serenity on his face that was

absolutely magnetic. But it was his lips I liked the best. They were quite curvy for a man and they turned slightly upward at the corners, as though the slightest bit of provocation would result in an eager smile.

It had been years since I'd noticed such things and, suddenly, I felt a pang of guilt. How could I find this man so incredibly attractive when I was married and the mother of two? How could I be so shallow? Why wasn't I evolved enough to put the physical appeal aside and turn my attention to all the wonderful things Joe could teach me? I'd run into the same problem ten years ago when I'd first met him and here I was, still behaving like a star-struck teenager.

Joe must have sensed my angst. "You okay?" he asked casually, even though I knew nothing he asked was ever casual. There was a clear and definite purpose to every subject Joe brought up and I knew he'd never let me get away with skirting the issue.

I stood at the water's edge and allowed a renegade wave to sweep across my bare feet. "Oh, Joe," I sighed, "I'm screwing this up again. I'm feeling really guilty about being here with you."

"Why is that?" he asked, and there was absolutely no emotion in his voice.

"Because I'm falling in love with you again," I admitted miserably. "I mean, I know our relationship is supposed to be pure and innocent and chaste and all that," I hastened to add, "but I'm starting to have feelings for you that aren't at all chaste." I could not believe I actually said that. How embarrassing. "I'm a horrible person, Joe," I went on. "I keep asking myself why Jim can't be more like you . . . gentle and patient and wise and non-judgmental."

"How do you know he's not?" Joe asked quietly.

"Because I'm married to him," I shot back a little too quickly. I should have known Joe was only baiting me, which seemed to be his preferred method of teaching me whatever it was he wanted me to learn at the moment.

Joe leaned back against a giant boulder of the jetty and my breath caught in my throat from the way he looked in the soft, golden, afternoon sun. "First of all," Joe began, "All those feelings that are suddenly waking up and washing over you have absolutely nothing to do with a physical attraction to me. Got that? So, stop with the guilt, okay?"

"Well, what else could it be?" I asked.

"It's simply love coming back into your heart," he said reverently as another wave washed over my feet and hissed across the sand. "And you're confused by that because it's been so long since you've allowed any real love into your heart."

I didn't know what to say. "Oh," was all I could manage.

"And as for wanting Jim to be a better man," Joe continued, "you can only help him by letting go and becoming a happier person yourself. Stop trying to fix him and concentrate instead on healing yourself. Step back and give him the space he needs to show you who he really is. Stop counting his drinks and watching the clock and fantasizing about what he might be doing when you're not around." We were both quiet while several more waves swirled around my feet. "Stop running his life, Christine," Joe urged, and though I was annoyed, I also knew that he was right. I'd grown rigid and controlling over the years and instead of making things better, it was destroying our relationship. I don't know how I knew that all of a sudden, but I did. Maybe it was osmosis or something.

"Did you know that Jim says a prayer for you every night?" Joe said in a tone so soft that I barely heard him. The words touched me deeply and I immediately felt something physically shift in my heart, like the underground movement of rocks in an earthquake.

"He does?" I said in a tiny voice. "What does he pray for?"

"That's privileged information."

"Oh. Sorry. It's just that . . ." I couldn't finish because big balloons of emotion were welling up within me, dwarfing my powers of speech.

"Go on," Joe encouraged.

I began to weep. "It's just that, I didn't know he still cared that much," I cried. "I mean, that's just about the sweetest, most romantic thing a man has ever done for me."

Joe stayed quiet while I mulled this over. Imagine, I thought, a man who prayed for his wife—a wife who nagged and badgered him over all kinds of insignificant things. That amazed me, but there was still one thing that bothered me. Not all of my concerns had been trivial or irrelevant and, though Jim prayed for me, he had also done some hurtful things over the years. It was hard, maybe even impossible for me to forget some of those incidences. What was I supposed to do about that?

"What do I do with my resentment, Joe?" I asked timidly. Joe's face softened with compassion as I asked this most difficult question. "How do I give up the grudge for the things he's already done in the past?"

Wordlessly, Joe held out both hands and, meekly, I took them.

"You give your resentments to me," he murmured softly. "That's the only way to get rid of them. Just whisper them in my ear—even when you think I'm not there to listen—and I'll dispose of them for you."

"Really? That's it?" I asked hopefully. "You mean, I haven't ruined everything? You mean, there's still a chance to make things right between Jim and me?"

"It's not as far gone as you think," Joe said earnestly. "You just got carried away in the role of 'wife'. You gave up on yourself and started focusing on everyone else instead, especially on their shortcomings. That's always been your biggest problem."

"So what should I do?" I pleaded. "Give me something concrete, okay?"

He laughed at that. "Okay," he agreed. "You've got to find your 'self' again before things can improve. I want you to go home and clear out a space for yourself somewhere in the house. I know the house is small, so it doesn't have to be a whole room, just a corner or an area that is yours and yours alone. Personalize it with the things you hold dear, you know, that blue throw-rug you love so much, the hand-painted vase your sister gave you, even your old nurse's cap if you can find it."

I rolled my eyes. "What good is that going to do?

As usual, Joe was infinitely patient with me. "Do you remember when we worked together ten years ago?" he asked. "Remember when I had you clean out your closet and you whined and complained all the way through it?"

I winced at the memory. "How could I forget?" I said, heaving a sigh. "And you were right. I did need to scale down and get rid of a lot of things that were cluttering up my life," I conceded. "But that's not the case any more."

"I know," he said. "This time I want you to beef up your living space a little. Stop giving up things so easily. You need to rope off some time and some space that is just for you instead of giving it all away in the name of marriage. Jim will understand. He's a good man. You just have to start putting some faith in him again. Sit back and watch what he becomes in the space that you give him. My guess is that he won't disappoint you."

"Your guess?" I said. "You have to guess? You don't *know* how Jim will react?"

Joe looked genuinely wounded when I said that and it wasn't hard to understand why. Once again, I had doubted him and I suppose he'd had a belly full of that over the years. I started to rephrase my comment, but Joe was already speaking.

"There's a little something called 'free will' involved here," he said. "I wish everybody would try to remember that. I don't control everything. I'm just there for you and for everybody else, kind of like a rescue worker showing you the way out, but nothing says you have to follow me. That's an individual decision. That's all I'm saying."

"I'm sorry, Joe," I murmured. "I'm always insulting you and you're always just trying to help. Can you forgive me?"

Joe didn't answer right away. He pushed off
from the rock he'd been leaning against and
walked over to the smooth sand that had been
left behind by the low tide. He picked up a
piece of driftwood and began writing.

"I'll do better than that." He grinned. "I'll
write out some reminders for you." He began
etching words into the sand as he spoke. "You
know, just a few pointers on everything we've
covered so far."

I watched in amazement as he wrote in the
most exquisite penmanship I'd ever seen:

Christine's Recipe for Romance

1. *Remember that you didn't fall out of
   love with your husband or your job.
   You fell out of love with yourself.*
2. *If you want to know what your purpose
   is, look in the mirror.*
3. *Suffering is not a requirement for losing
   weight.*
4. *Revel in the fact that you are an artist,
   a shaman, a healer.*

The words were profound and I quickly tried
to memorize them as several ocean waves swept
dangerously close to them. "Joe!" I exclaimed,
"Why did you write them in the sand? The
ocean's going to wash them away!"

Unflinching, Joe stood back and watched the waves encroach upon his cherished words, erasing every last trace of them.

"There's no such thing as security," he said, smiling. "You need to learn that too."

SEVEN

In the days that followed, a number of changes began to take place, some of them subtle, others more obvious. Without any prompting from me, Joey and Gracie chose Thursday as the day they volunteered to forego all extracurricular activities from now on because being at home was actually 'more fun'. Imagine that. I wondered if it had anything to do with the fact that I was feeling more relaxed these days and perhaps I was a little easier to be around. It was an intriguing possibility.

Jim and I also made changes in our schedules so that we could spend that time together as a family. We experimented with different dinner choices, sometimes cooking a meal together and at other times, opting for take-out. Occasionally, we played board games after dinner and oftentimes, we simply watched television together. A powerful feeling of utter contentment sneaked up on me one night as I studied my family in the ghostly glow of the television when they didn't know I was looking. This cozy, little scene was a miracle I had once despaired of, yet suddenly, it was occurring in my own living room each and every Thursday night. Though it was only one day out of seven, it was enough for now.

In a fit of new and unbridled optimism, I took Jim up on his offer to do the grocery shopping between tutoring sessions. Never before had I been willing to trust that he would get the right brand of bleach or enough fresh vegetables, but for some reason, I now began to see the insignificance of such minor details. For once, I had actually become willing to let go of all of the control over the shopping and to accept a little help from my partner. Maybe it doesn't sound like a big deal, but in the context of our usual arrangements, this represented an enormous surrender on my part.

It's embarrassing to admit, but there were times when Jim brought home totally different brands that were not only less expensive, but far superior to the ones I usually bought. He even proved to be a savvier shopper than I, saving more money with coupons than I had thought

possible. The most impressive thing though, was
that he never said a word about it. I just
discovered it when I balanced the checkbook
and that sort of warmed my heart. If the shoe
had been on the other foot . . . well, I don't know
if I would have been quite so gracious.

I also began to let the laundry pile up instead
of forcing myself to stay ahead of it late at night
when I was already exhausted from a full day of
work and family. I cut down to running the
washing machine every other day and I did it
earlier in the evening. Now, when I took clothes
out of the dryer, I let the kids get involved in
helping and we made a game out of sorting and
folding it. It seemed incredible to me that there
had once been a time when I hadn't trusted
anyone to do such chores to my liking. Now
that I was learning to be a little more flexible, I
found that it made my life infinitely easier. I
was astonished to learn that the world didn't
end if towels and sheets weren't folded exactly
the way my mother had taught me to do it, and
that it was just as easy to sleep in a bed that had
been made up without hospital corners. I
wondered why I'd never realized these things
before.

At night, after Jim left to play in the band, I
gathered Gracie and Joey together on the couch
and read stories to them before bedtime. Though
they were both old enough to read books on

their own, all three of us found something comforting and maybe even a little magical, about sharing such a calm and relaxing ritual. It seemed to infuse them with a sense of security, while strengthening my maternal bond with them at the same time.

Even work was becoming more bearable. For one thing, I discovered that putting my focus on the parts of my job that were still satisfying, helped to minimize my discontent with the bureaucracy. I poured most of my energy into teaching my patients about their injuries and/or illnesses, while maintaining some hands-on care at the same time. It didn't lessen the amount of paperwork or administrative nonsense that went on, but it helped me to notice it less. As I became more involved with the patients on our unit, I also noticed that some of the younger nurses were gravitating toward me and seeking my advice. I shuddered to think that there had been a time when I'd begrudged sharing my expertise with them because I had simply been too overwhelmed with my own agenda to be concerned with theirs.

Now that I saw myself as a healer first and an employee second, I was a lot more generous with my time. After more than two decades in this profession, I finally knew with great confidence who and what I was, and that was all that mattered. If the bureaucracy didn't like

it, that was their privilege. The funny thing was
that as I grew stronger in my own beliefs about
myself, the very people who used to nit-pick
and harass me suddenly began backing off. It
was fascinating.

Even food had become less and less
important, perhaps because I no longer felt so
empty. People began noticing that I was losing
weight even before I noticed it myself, and that
was truly miraculous. Ordinarily, I was painfully
aware of every ounce of fluctuation in my weight,
but these days it just didn't seem all that
important. Paradoxically, the more I ignored the
scale, the slimmer I became. I wondered if this
was what Joe had meant when he told me that
suffering wasn't a necessary part of losing weight.
Now that I wasn't obsessing over diets and calories
and fat grams, I had a reserve of unused energy
available to me for far more productive purposes.

I put my renewed stamina to good use. One
Friday evening when Jim was playing in the band
and the kids were at a neighbor's house for an
end of summer sleep-over with their friends, I
was delighted to find that I had an entire,
undisturbed evening all to myself. Inspired, I
decided to construct that personal space in my
home that Joe had so strongly encouraged.

I made a quick trip to the local *Pier One* and
bought an inexpensive white wicker desk with a
matching chair and placed them in a tiny, unused

corner of the dining room. Next, I rummaged through the garage until I found the silk screen I'd had when I was single, and set it up behind the desk, ensuring myself a little privacy. I also found the blue throw rug Joe had mentioned and placed it beside the chair. I added a couple of scented candles, a beautiful, unused journal I'd received as a gift three years ago, and a couple of novels I'd been trying to find the time to read since 1994. I felt a little like *Humpty-Dumpty* as I picked up some long-forgotten pieces of my past and began putting them back together again.

The time flew as I searched for meaningful artifacts from my life and added them to my little sanctuary. On the top shelf of my closet, buried behind some dust-covered boxes of outdated shoes and purses, I spotted my original nurse's cap. It was the one I'd received during our capping ceremony a million years ago when I was a student nurse. Tenderly, I picked it up and examined the little piece of organdy as though it were a fossil that might crumble under even the slightest touch. Though it resembled an upside-down cupcake and probably weighed less than an ounce, it had once been laden with meaning.

Things had changed so drastically since those days, I thought, and we never saw it coming. It was a different era then when money and insurance coverage were not even an issue and the patients' welfare was the hospital's top priority. Had there really been such a time of innocence? A wave of nostalgia swept over me and I closed my eyes. I felt myself transported back to the days when a simple thing like a nurse's cap had been a symbol of pride, a rite of passage, a tribute to a truly noble profession.

Suddenly, I was back in that softly lit room again where fifty student nurses knelt with heads bowed, each holding a single, white candle in trembling, young hands. Though in reality, I was standing in the bedroom that I now shared with my husband, I somehow felt the same palpable reverence of that night as if no time at all had passed. I could have sworn I even felt the butterfly weight of the organdy cap being placed on my head and pinned to my upswept, chestnut-colored hair.

"The past always looks much better in retrospect," someone was saying from far off in the distance and I opened my eyes to find Joe standing before me. "And you wouldn't want to go back to the way it was anyway," he added, "because that would eliminate the idea of progress."

"But I think it was better in those days," I whispered as though I were still in the middle of a capping ceremony.

"Not necessarily," Joe said wistfully. "Just different. And simpler, maybe. But that doesn't always add up to 'better'."

"Where have you been?" I blurted out, no longer the slightest bit interested in the state of the health care system. "I've missed you."

"I know," he said, and somehow it didn't sound the tiniest bit egotistical. I wondered how he did that.

"Hey, I have a question for you," I said, suddenly remembering the afternoon we'd spent on Sandy Hook.

"Shoot."

"How come you only gave me four instructions this time instead of six like the last time? And what was all that business about there being no such thing as security? That spooked me a little. Explain please."

Joe looked amused as he sat down on the foot of the bed. Without knowing why, I lowered myself onto the floor and sat at his feet like an adoring child. For some reason, I felt really comfortable that way.

"Listen to me carefully, Christine," Joe began, and his voice took on an almost somber tone. "The more evolved you get, the more general are the principles you need to remember. You see, as people grow and become more comfortable with their own spirituality, the lines between individuals begin to blur and that's good. You get closer and closer to realizing that, in essence, we are all the very same person. The first time I had to give you more specific instructions because you weren't ready to process the things I've tried to teach you this time."

I was quiet while I tried to absorb the magnitude of Joe's words. "Will there be a next time?" I wanted to know.

"Maybe," he said and his tone was non-committal. "You see, that's what I meant about there being no such thing as security, Christine. There is, but it's not the kind most people are looking for. You don't find security in things or in money or in promises. You find it in your heart, in living each day so that it really counts, and you find it when you reach out to someone else, whether that means helping them or allowing them to help you. It's all the same thing. Goodwill toward one another is the greatest form of security there is."

"But what about people who aren't that evolved yet?" I asked. "People who think it's cool to steal or kill or cause trouble?"

"That's what I call 'free will run riot'," Joe answered sadly. "I created *free*-will in order to promote *good*-will, but you're right, not everyone sees it that way." He stared silently out the window and looked up at the stars for what seemed an unusually long time. " . . . And then they blame me for letting awful things happen," he continued as if there had been no pause in the dialogue. "They actually think that I cause the catastrophes and they demand to know what kind of a 'God' would do such a thing. Most people still don't understand that I gave the gift of free will with no strings attached. I have faith in each and every one of you to do the right thing, no matter how many times a person falls off the path or misuses that gift."

I didn't know what to say. It disturbed me to see Joe look as burdened and troubled as he did at that moment. I looked into his russet eyes and was surprised to see that they were swimming in unshed tears. Suddenly, I wanted more than anything to console this man who spent all of his time comforting and guiding others.

Like a confused child trying to soothe an anguished parent, I put my hand on Joe's knee. "I'll never blame you for anything again, Joe," I said. "It must be terrible to work so hard at helping people, only to have them turn their backs on you when the chips are down."

"Thank you, Christine," he said quietly. A ghost of a smile crossed his lips and then he patted my hand, stood up, and let himself out.

EIGHT

After Joe left, I stayed in the bedroom and listened to the peace and quiet he had left in his wake. It was ironic, I thought, now that I had all the privacy and solitude I'd been yearning for, suddenly, I didn't want to be alone. Then I got an idea. Why not go down to the club where Jim was playing tonight and surprise him? It would be good to feel like an actively engaged woman again instead of the frumpy, regimented, lackluster person I'd allowed myself to become over the years.

I pulled a freshly laundered pink bath sheet from my private stock that I usually reserved for company only, and draped it over the towel rack. Next, I dug through my top drawer until I found the French soaps Jim had given me on my birthday, the ones I was never quite in the mood to use. Well, I was in the mood now.

I took my time in the shower, a luxury in and of itself, and reveled in the rich, floral scent of the soap. Afterward, I sat on a chair and smoothed a creamy body lotion onto my damp skin, an extravagance I usually denied myself for the sake of time.

I was pleasantly surprised to find that just about everything in my closet was too big for me all of a sudden and I refused to be annoyed by that. Then I remembered a pair of jeans I'd bought in an impossibly small size a few years ago when I'd been trying to motivate myself to diet. I found them crammed into a corner of the closet and I slipped into them with room to spare. It was a wonderful feeling. Next, I pulled on a mauve T-shirt that had shrunk drastically in the wash and I was thrilled to find that it now fit quite flatteringly. I added a sparkly belt, matching sandals, a silver bracelet, a touch of make up, and I was ready for my first public appearance at the club in years.

I called and left my cell phone number with my neighbor in case the kids needed me for anything. Once that was taken care of, I mentally metamorphosed into a more serene and mature version of Christine Moore, on her way to spend a lovely evening in the company of a very handsome and talented musician whose music had always intrigued her.

Harold's Pub was cool, smoky, and dimly lit, just as I remembered. In fact, it was *exactly* the way I remembered it. The only thing that was noticeably different now was, well, me. Okay, that and the fact that the bouncers looked like they would never even remotely consider carding me. That part was different, for sure.

I liked the changes I was noticing in myself. I felt a new sense of confidence as I made my way through the smoky haze toward an empty chair that was set off to the side of the stage. I was delighted to find that even in the presence of so many dewy, creamy complexions and perfect figures, I suddenly did not feel the least bit intimidated or out of place. Instead of feeling ridiculous or threatened by the young girls who blatantly flirted with my husband, I now felt compassion for all they would have to go through before they ever arrived at the graceful and sophisticated stage in life that I felt I had finally grown into. Well, what do you know? Christine Moore MaGuire of Neptune City, New Jersey was finally, at long last, at peace with herself.

Maybe life was fair after all.

The band was just finishing a number that I didn't recognize and unobtrusively, I took my seat in the crowd. I noticed that the keyboard player nudged Jim and I smiled shyly when my husband did a double take at the sight of me. Without a word, Jim then seated himself on the stool at center stage and the lights dimmed to almost blackout proportions. He picked up his saxophone and began playing a haunting version of a little known song he'd written just for me shortly before we were married.

I felt a red-hot rush of embarrassment creep up my neck and stain my cheeks when I recognized the intimacy of what he was saying with his music. It was as though Jim was proclaiming his love for me in front of a couple of hundred strangers and I was flattered to no end. I felt myself beaming in the dim glow of the stage lights and my heart swelled with pride because this man I was married to was such an incredible artist.

"Don't forget that you're an artist, too," someone murmured next to my ear and I turned, but no one was there.

The guys in the band offered to pack up the equipment after the club closed, allowing Jim and me to leave a little early. We left Jim's van in the parking lot for their purposes and went home together in my car, like two lovers who were out on a date.

I slid into the passenger seat, content to relinquish the steering wheel to Jim while I searched for a suitable song on the radio. Fat, heavy raindrops began to dot the windshield as we pulled onto State Highway #35 and by the time we reached the 'Welcome to Neptune City' sign, thunder was shattering the late night silence and lightening was piercing the thick, muggy sky.

We parked in the driveway and ran through the rain into the shelter of our darkened living room. A flash of lightening lit up the room and instinctively, I nestled my face into Jim's shoulder. The next thing I knew, Jim was cupping my face in his graceful, musician's hands and he began kissing me in a way I had feared might never happen again.

On a lark, I suggested we drag the mattress off our bed and sleep in the living room tonight, watching what would likely be the last of the summer storms. It turned out to be an inspired idea.

We talked late into the night, while thunder and lightening punctuated our heartfelt words and thoughts. There was something comforting about the cloak of darkness surrounding us. It made it easier for us to communicate honestly, providing refuge from the painful emotions that were written across our faces. It had been far too long since we'd talked like this, and I began to sense the emergence of a brand new intimacy that was budding between us.

In the cover of darkness, I found the courage to let go of all my defenses and I apologized for being so cold and controlling of Jim sometimes. I told him that I understood myself much better these days and that my tension and irritability had been the result of my own unhappiness with myself. I knew now that it had little or nothing to do with his behavior. I promised that from now on, I would spend a lot more time looking at my own flaws and defects instead of automatically transferring my frustrations onto him.

After I was done, there was a long silence and it wasn't until the next lightening strike that I saw tears glistening on my husband's cheek.

Then it was his turn. I discovered things about Jim that night that never would have been revealed in the harsh light of day. I found out that he had been afraid of my disapproval, scared that he wasn't living up to my expectations as a husband or as a father to our children. I was amazed to learn that he suffered similar insecurities to mine about his talents, his relationship skills, and, most surprisingly, his sexual appeal. He apologized for his disappointing career path and admitted that he really didn't blame me for resenting the fact that I'd had to go back to work to make ends meet.

"I don't resent working any more," I said, and I meant it. We both lay there quietly through a few more claps of thunder and I thought about all the misery that had been caused by a hidden culprit called miscommunication.

"I've been so unfair to you, Jim," I said solemnly. "How did you stand me? I mean, really. What kept you from picking up and leaving?"

I felt his hand grasp mine underneath the sheet and an odd look crossed his face. "I'd never leave you, Christine," he said in a voice that was taut with emotion.

"Really?" I was incredulous. "Never? Why not?"

He hesitated for a fraction of a second. "There's something I never told you," he said, "because I was afraid you might think I was crazy."

"I'd never think that," I said softly.

He squeezed my hand and went on tentatively. "About ten years ago, right around the time I met you," he began, "I met this guy. Well, he wasn't just *any* guy." He paused. "He was God."

I gasped. I couldn't help it. I was shocked. "Go on," I said, trying to keep my voice calm.

Jim looked anxious, but he courageously carried on anyway. "Well, he told me that you were the one for me," he continued. "He said that maybe we'd learn some painful lessons from each other, but that you were the one woman in the world who I was meant to travel through this life with." He was quiet then and I waited. "That's all I ever needed to know," he finished. "I've been in it for the long run ever since."

My heart was in my throat and it rendered me speechless. Joe had come to Jim. It was true. And that's why Joe had winked at me when Jim and I first got together. He was giving his approval after all. Well, what do you know?

Out of the blue, I felt that old attraction coming back again, a longing I'd not had for my husband in years. Apparently, the feeling was mutual because Jim leaned over then and kissed me and when he did, my heart cracked open and ten years of stifled love came spilling out.

Later, as we lay staring out at the storm, Jim told me that a producer from a new, late–night talk show that was in the works, had been at the club tonight. He had been looking for a band to complement the new host of the show and apparently he had liked what he'd heard. Jim and the band had an audition scheduled for tomorrow in New York and if things went well, they were promised a salary that surpassed the dreams Jim had long ago put to rest.

The irony is that, all of a sudden, it didn't matter. What mattered was that I loved my husband again and that we had two beautiful, healthy children and a home and a wonderful life together. For once, money was actually meaningless. I fell asleep in my husband's arms and when we awoke, our bond had somehow grown even stronger.

The morning was clear and bright with not

even a hint of the thunderstorm that had raged throughout the night. It was my weekend off so Jim and I shared a leisurely breakfast together and then I drove him to the train station in Belmar. I kissed him for luck, then stood on the platform and watched until his northbound train disappeared into the distance toward the long overdue promise of success.

The kids wouldn't be home till after nine, so I stopped for coffee and then decided that I still had time to go for a pleasant jog along the beach. Though it was a bit of a drive, I wanted to run on Sandy Hook this morning. There was something about the vastness of that place and its untouched, rugged beauty that drew me there. Thirty minutes later, I was doing stretches beside my car and looking out at the shimmering horizon of a glorious, September morning.

I broke into a slow and steady jog as I watched the seagulls go into a feeding frenzy for the chum on the back of a lone fishing boat a few hundred yards out. Everything felt so right that I wasn't the least bit surprised when I heard the sound of footsteps running alongside of me. I didn't even have to look. I knew Joe would show up again.

"Good morning," he called, not even panting.

"Good morning," I called back, beaming.

"I'm glad to see you looking so happy, Christine," he said without breaking his easy stride. "I take it you and Jim had a chance to straighten things out a bit, right?"

"Right you are," I laughed. Then I remembered what Jim had said last night and I stopped abruptly. "So, you came to Jim, too," I said, panting. "Why didn't you tell me?"

Joe smirked boyishly. "Because I knew he'd tell you in his own good time."

I stood still for a moment and studied Joe's beautiful face. He looked positively jubilant. "You look so good, Joe," I said sincerely. "You're actually glowing."

"Seeing people together again does wonders for my spirit," he agreed.

I studied his face a moment longer in the golden glow of morning, trying to memorize the sparkle, the enthusiasm, and the love that emanated from him. "Thank you for showing me the way again," I murmured softly.

"My pleasure."

"You're going to leave now, aren't you?" I asked, though I already knew the answer. I don't know how I knew that my time was up, but I did.

Joe nodded. "You can handle it from here, Christine. I have faith in you."

With that, he reached for my hand, brought it to his curvy lips, and planted a long, warm kiss across my knuckles.

"No tangible proof this time?" I asked, hoping

he'd leave me with some kind of a token of our time together.

Joe just smiled and winked and I watched him walk up the beach toward his Harley. I stayed put till I heard the rumble of the engine and I saw him raise his hand in the air as he gave me a thumbs up signal. Then, like a shooting star, he took off across the parking lot and headed south toward the mainland.

Saddened, I turned back toward the sea and stared out across the glimmering water. Eventually, my gaze fell upon the smooth, wet sand at the water's edge. Something had been etched there and, even though the waves were swirling across it, they'd had no effect on the imprint. Curious, I walked toward it and what I saw took my breath away.

The outline of an enormous heart with an arrow through it stared back at me and, written inside were the words:

Joe loves Christine. Forever.

34845206R00073

Made in the USA
Middletown, DE
07 September 2016